For my … Linda

THE DEVIL SPINNERS

MARGIT HESTHAMMAR

Much love always,
Mag

FriesenPress
One Printers Way
Altona, MB R0G 0B0
Canada

www.friesenpress.com

First Edition — 2024

Cover design by Margit Hesthammar
Design execution by Romana Zeman
Author photo by Jeff Hesthammer

ISBN
978-1-03-830101-7 (Hardcover)
978-1-03-830100-0 (Paperback)
978-1-03-830102-4 (eBook)

Fiction, Short Stories (Single Author)

Distributed to the trade by The Ingram Book Company

For my beloved husband, Chris Welsby

CONTENTS

THE STICKINESS FACTOR

THE STICKINESS FACTOR

The day begins with great promise. I have a story to write and I'm ready to go. The plants are watered, the dishes are done, the place is neat as a pin. I have five whole hours before I have to leave for work, and I even have an idea.

I've been studying residual stickiness in dead relationships—the kind that are over but never quite end. I work in a bar, so I witness real-life stickiness every day. The effects are self-evident: no one gets on with their lives. The causes are more mysterious. Why is it that some people can't bring themselves to pull the final pin? Is it the inconvenience of change? Inertia? Fierce attachment? Or is it the times? Are their minds so scattered by devices that they simply forget they were breaking up?

My plan is to throw a few characters together, see who sticks once the thrill is gone, and document my observations.

I write STORY at the top of the page and consider my opening line. The tense is holding me up. Past or present—always a challenge. Past carries more authority; present packs more of a punch.

I have just decided on present when there's a knock on my door. I am briefly jolted, but resolute. I have learned to ignore the door.

Another knock, more assertive this time. *Damn.* I tiptoe to the peephole: Two policemen. *What the...?*

I assume they've got the wrong address and decide to deal with it now. Cops always come back later and I don't want half my brain on hold, wondering when. Besides, my place looks great and I have nothing to hide.

I open the door. The taller of the two is a blond, gym-built type. He scans the apartment as he makes the introductions and doesn't look at me. The shorter man is dark and a little on the husky side. He looks me up and down while they show me their IDs.

"We're looking for Samuel William Taylor," says the blond one. "Is he home?"

"I have no idea," I say. "Why are you looking for him here?"

"Is this not his address?"

"No. Sam hasn't lived here for years. How did you get my address?"

"It's on his driver's license."

I vow to murder Sam when I see him next. The last time I confronted him he swore he'd stopped using my address for bills and tickets and ladies he wasn't sure of. For four years now, he's been using my number as a buffer service. Only last week I spent an hour on the phone with his mother, who still calls to find out if he's eating.

"Well, he doesn't live here," I say, "but you're welcome to look around if you like."

They give the place a cursory glance; it's clear I'm the only one there.

"Can you tell us where he does live then?" asks the blond one.

"I don't think he has a place right now. He's been staying with different friends." This is not strictly true, but I can't tell them where he is if he's actually in trouble. "Can you tell me why you're looking for him?"

"Yeah—hit and run, impaired, dangerous driving, refusal to blow, failure to appear."

"*Sam?*" I say.

"Samuel William Taylor," he says.

"Gosh," I say. "That doesn't sound like him." Actually, it doesn't. I explain that Sam's in the habit of using my address when he doesn't have one of his own. They tell me I should be careful who I give my address to and there are penalties for harbouring criminals. (*Criminals?*) Then they ask me to tell Sam there's a warrant out for his arrest and he better get down to the courthouse if he wants to avoid spending time in jail. I tell them I'll put out the word and they leave.

I go back to the table and sit down. *Damn that Sam.* This is worse than if I'd ignored the door. Now I've got Sam in my head, and the police, and the job of tracking Sam down. It's his own fault. I should let the chips fall. But then I picture the wounded look he gets if he thinks for half a second you don't have his back. I hate that look.

I actually can't figure it. Sam is not the hit-and-run type. He's not even the hit type. In fifteen years I've never known Sam to hit so much as a wrong note on the road. Even after four pints and three B & B's, he's an ace driver.

It's no good pretending I'm going to ignore this. I can't even remember where I was in my story. Then I remember—stuck on the first line. *What story?*

Damn that Sam. I start hunting for his address. I know he has a little hole-in-the-wall somewhere, but I haven't seen it yet. It's not worth visiting anywhere Sam lives till he's been there at least six months. My calculations tell me he's been in his latest place for under three. Which means it will still be a room full of boxes with a foamy in the cupboard and a giant sound system in the middle of the floor.

Sam has the best sound system of anyone I know. Music is his thing.

It doesn't pay the rent, though. He works on towboats when he works, and when he's between places he stays at the Ivanhoe on Main Street. But cheap hotels on Main Street are where the flotsam of the sea end up, and he's always a little nervous about getting stuck there. Besides, it's not every woman who jumps at the chance to hang out on skid row.

Sam is dedicated to a life of desperation. I think he finds it romantic. Unlike "most men," however, his style is anything but quiet. He teeters loudly on the edge and complains. For Sam, whining is performance art—a blend of stand-up, country and bad opera.

As I said, he works on towboats, but generally only long enough to collect pogey. And there's always one main bad guy—usually the skipper—who gives him a great reason to quit: "Gabe," he'll say, "I'm working on a goddam mousetrap. Two weeks with this guy and I'm ready to put my head in the oven. You know what he says when we're tying up in Port Hardy? Just as we're going ashore? First time off in ten days? He says 'Limit yourselves to two beers apiece, boys, and be back by 11:00. We're shipping out tonight instead of tomorrow.'

"And why are we all of a sudden shipping out early? Because he wants to save time so the company won't have to pay us an extra day. And why do we have to leave in the middle of the night? Because he wants the tide going with us through Seymour Narrows. Which it would be if we left the next day, as planned—with the small added benefit of daylight. But *oh* no, we have to ship out in the dark.

"Two beers—it's not even worth going ashore. You spend ten days on a mousetrap with six guys and no booze. Everyone's drinking coffee at triple-speed. Everyone's wired. Half a dozen hair triggers holding fire for this one night out and the skipper tells us to be back by 11:00."

Of course there's a mutiny, led by Sam. And of course they can't fire the whole crew, at least not till they're back in Vancouver, by which time Sam has worked long enough to collect pogey.

After pogey, he might transfer to welfare for a while, which he really can't live on. He'll get thin and hungry looking till some woman comes along and shapes him up. The man is perennially up for adoption. Having done a little stretch with him myself, I can testify to his talent—Sam could find the mother in a sheet of drywall.

Great promise, though. He played a fabulous trumpet when I first met him. I always thought he was going to become a professional musician. But he can't keep his lip because his trumpet is always in the pawnshop. "Had to 'hawnk' my horn again, Gabe," he says. Right before he asks me to float him another beer.

***

So here I am, stuck with the task of tracking Sam down, knowing he won't actually be living in his hole-in-the-wall unless he's between women, and knowing after several tries that his phone, as usual, is not charged. I have one option, which is to call his current lady friends. Which I would rather not do. Women get violent around Sam sooner or later—the stickiness factor—and I'm not up-to-date on who's sticky these days. He never fills me in till it makes a good story.

I think of Randy Rockwell—a possibility, though he told me she put a boulder through his windshield a couple of months ago. Sam drives a block-long '67 Cadillac that he sometimes sleeps in, but I don't know if it's parked or on the road right now.

Then I remember the hit-and-run. Well, it *was* on the road

yesterday. I should call Randy—Sam calls her Rocky now—but I'm not ready for it. She runs hot and cold with me. Hot if they're on, cold if they're off. Because I've known Sam forever, she can't decide if I'm a threat—which I'm not—but I can't reassure her because she pretends not to care.

Stickiness denied. Irritating at the best of times; impossible when the parties are not officially an item. I decide to leave Rocky to last and make a note to add "Premature Stickiness" to my taxonomy. Or "Fantasy Residue." I'll sort it out later.

Next I think of Veronica Head-Waring. Sam calls her Ronnie Red-Herring, "Red" for short, because her hair is on the red side. Ronnie prefers Veronica and insists she's a blond. Sam has been switch-hitting between Rocky and Ronnie for the past few months, driving them both crazy. Unfortunately, they only live three blocks apart and Sam doesn't have the sense to park his caddie in another neighbourhood. So they both always know when he's with the other.

Ronnie has a shorter fuse than Rocky and she put a boulder through Sam's windshield a month after Rocky did. She's by far the stickiest woman on his trap line. Sam is furious because he's lost credibility with the insurance company and claims he's getting spider-vision from trying to see the road.

Unlike Rocky, Ronnie has no shame whatsoever. She'll come into Crawley's and grill me for an hour on every little thing Sam has said or done since she saw him last. Then she'll be furious because I know more than she does. When I remind her that I'm the bartender at his local pub and therefore can't help seeing him practically every day, she just sniffs and flips her hair. I decide to leave her to last too.

I consider calling Angela Moody. She and Sam hang out when Angela needs help watching her current boyfriend. Sam's an imaginary spare for her—strictly a decoy—and she's a kinky sideline for Sam—safely spoken for, strictly non-stick. They always sit by the door while Angela waits for her true love to show up. That way he'll have to walk right by her, coming or going. When he comes in, she smiles radiantly ("What do you think, Sam, did I look too happy to see him? Did I look too eager? *Crap!*"). Then she watches him talking to other women and waits to find out if he's going to take her home. Sam says she's a pain-collector. "Watching Angela Moody watching her boyfriend is like watching someone rolling around on broken glass," he says. "You don't want to get too close."

Sam feels safe as long as the boyfriend is in the neighbourhood. Ninety percent of Angela's attention—and the broken glass—are aimed at him. But if the boyfriend says goodbye and leaves, ("Bye!" she'll wave, with a tinkly little laugh), or worse, if he says goodbye and leaves with another woman, it's time to evacuate. Sam pretends to head for the men's room and sneaks out the back way. "Time to clear out," he'll say. "The shards are gonna fly." And for the next twenty minutes anyone in Angela's vicinity will look like they're catching a face-full.

Sam says Angela and her boyfriend only ever had one date, and that was over a year ago. Residual stickiness would be more like a lifestyle choice with her. I glance at my notes. Hard to classify year-old unrequited stickiness; any first-date residue would have evaporated months ago. I make a note to add Crazy Glue to my taxonomy.

There's no answer when I call Angela, so I try Kristina, who is also a server at Crawley's. She and Sam have a nice now-and-again thing. I like Kris. She grew up in Czechia with four brothers and knows about men. Or at least, accepts them. She says the best way to deal with men is to enjoy the chemistry while it lasts, brotherize them as soon as possible after that, and never, ever become the main squeeze. It sounds much better with the Czech accent.

"Save your heart for the puppies and kittens," she says. "Is for the best. The men they struggle, you know? Hard-wired at eight weeks already—did you know this? *While they are still in the womb!* I read in a science book. Can you imagine? No bigger than a raspberry—a tiny *raspberry!*—when the testeronyk swoop in and kill the connection thingies in their brain. The poor men," she says fondly. Then she snorts. "Unless, of course, you want to make the babies. Then the *poor you!*" And she gives you a little hip-chuck and cracks up.

Kristina is Teflon Woman.

I dial her number. By some miracle she's home, but she hasn't seen Sam since last night. I ask who he was with, and she tells me he came in with Max, but Max left an hour before Sam.

I heave a long sigh. Max is an advanced drinker and purveyor of fine white powders who does his purveying in a noisily hush-hush way. Everyone knows about it, and everyone uses Max as a last resort, but because there's a lot of last-resort business at Crawley's, Max keeps pretty busy. He's been accident-prone since he lost his license (six charges of impaired) because he now goes everywhere on his bike. And he likes to hotdog around—no hands, screaming down Fourth at rush hour, tearing through red lights. He's usually covered in bruises, which makes him look thuggier than he really is.

I sigh again. If Sam was with Max and Max left first, there was no doubt some powder in the wind. Sam has only been ashore for a week, which means he's still burning money. He could be anywhere by now. He could have started a whole new trap line I haven't even met yet.

Sam is a snake for women. That's how his friends put it. "The man is a snake," says Dutch, his archrival and best friend. "I'm sitting on the patio at Gillie's with this new lady, and it's our first date. Well, we slept together once, but the point is, I liked her. So I asked her out on a real date. I got all cleaned up and borrowed a hundred bucks from Brad, and we're having a nice quiet time when Sam walks in.

"He comes right over, sits down at the table without asking, and tells her she's got a great nose. 'You got a great nose,' he says, and right away she's eating out of his hand. I'm sitting there like a schlump, watching him tell her what a great nose she has. Oh, and how he loves Kurt Vonnegut—she mentions she's reading some book by Kurt Vonnegut—and how he has this other book by Kurt Vonnegut, she should give him her number and he'll drop it by. And she does. She *does.* And by then I'm going *fuck you lady* and having nothing more to do with her, the bitch, but I've still got to sit there, right? I've still got to sit there because she's still legally my date, and I can't just walk out because then she and Sam will hang out and Sam will take her home. That's it. That's it on Sam. *Finito.* Next time I see him I get booked for murder."

Of course, the next time Sam and Dutch see each other, neither of them has a date and they both happen to be on the patio at Gillie's again. Dutch walks over to Sam's table, whips off his glasses and hucks them into the street—right under the wheels of a passing truck. Sam throws his wine in Dutch's face. Dutch tips Sam's table into his lap. The management breaks them up and kicks them out. So now it's them against the world and they have to make up because the night is young and they both still want to have supper and drink some more. They're quasi-friends again, as usual.

"A snake," says Dutch. Well, it's true in a way. Sam does have a way with women, though it's hard to say exactly why. He has a narrow, hunched-over body with oversized limbs, and he's so oddly put together you could never really call him handsome. But he's funny, and he has some good moves. And there's the music, of course.

I think the secret is that he sulks well. Women who have never administered so much as a bandage become healers around Sam.

So I've got some kind of lead—he was looking for substances, and probably women—but it's the worst possible lead I could have. Meanwhile, it's time to get ready for work.

I leave early so I can cruise by his place, but there's no answer when I buzz. So I leave a note on his door to call me at work.

The bar is busy and loud. I start at rush hour—4:00 p.m.—and for the next two hours I'm a blur. Crawley's has a horseshoe bar on the ground floor that loops through the middle of the room. There's stand-up capacity for ten around the shoe, twenty if people double up. At the end of the loop is the self-serve counter, which generally has a lineup of ten to fifteen, and beside that is the servers' counter. There are four servers on the floor, two upstairs and two down. Each is responsible for eight tables, and each table seats four in a pinch. Most nights there's a lineup around the block to get in.

I'm tending bar today, so I'm the one spinning inside the shoe. With the standers, the self-servers and the servers on the floor, I have about fifty orders coming at me at any given time. It is not a job for the lame of brain. Or limb. On the plus side, time flies and I never have to go to a gym.

When the rush subsides, I notice Max is sitting by the outside door. He's grinning, which is unusual. Max is a scowly German type who calls himself "The Sour Kraut" and makes a point of never smiling back.

I watch him get up and wander over to a group of men who are standing in the self-serve line. You can tell by his smirk that he's worked up a good story.

I'm too busy to leave the bar and I can't catch his eye, so I cock an ear and hear him say "...I gave them the license, and they went through the usual routine. It was day three of a four-day bender"—Max prides himself on keeping track—"so I refused to blow, and they charged me. I was supposed to show up for prints this morning—that is, Sammie Taylor was—but I slept in. I mean, can you believe it? I'm backing out of Safeway, I'm not even out of the parking lot, and I back into a cop car. I've been in the car for less than a minute and I hit a *parked cop.*

"I'm so surprised, first that I hit someone so soon, and second that I hit a cop, that I ram it into drive and step on it. Instinct, right? You see that little cherry and you gun it. Only now I'm so focused on the rear-view mirror that I forget to look ahead, and I smack head-on into the car in front of me. Which is also parked. Can you believe it? I swear that caddie of Sam's is the longest motherfucking car in the world. So there I am with nowhere to go, sandwiched between two cars that I've just rear-ended and front-ended.

"Talk about the fastest car chase in history—the cops don't even have to shift out of park. They just climb out of their car and stand there with their arms folded. Like they can't actually get what's just happened. I can't either.

"But here's the good part: I'm so guilty for trying to get away that I lean out and say, 'Hey guys, I'm too drunk to deal with this—the car just got away on me.' I actually *tell* the cops I'm too drunk to drive. They look at me like I'm the new arrival at the zoo. Then one of them opens my door and bows, like he's inviting the British ambassador to step this way. Thank God I was clean. All I had on me was Sammie's ID and two hundred bucks. So they book me for hit-and-run, dangerous driving, refusal to blow and impaired. I was supposed to go down for prints this morning—I mean, Sam Taylor was—but I didn't wake up till 3:00. Anyone seen Sammie today?"

I finish the lineup on fast-forward, then lean across the bar and yell, *"Max!!"* He looks up and I shout, *"Here! Now!!"*

His grin droops and he shuffles over. "Did you happen to see the address on that license, Max? It's mine, dammit, and I had a visit from two cops today, looking for Sam. Do you mean to say you haven't even found him yet? Am I hearing this right?? And how did you get his car and ID in the first place?"

Well, nobody likes a critic. Max looks righteously put-upon and explains that he got the car and ID from Sam because he was running a little errand for the guy, and how can he track him down when he never charges his phone?

I can't stand it. I ask the manager to take over and walk off the bar. Then I go upstairs to the office and start phoning. I finally track Sam down at Gillie's. Within five minutes he's at the bar, and for the rest of the night, he and Max and Mike Styles, the bar lawyer, are plotting strategies. Mike finally decides that Sam has to call the cops and tell them he's lost his car, keys and ID. It's a tricky business, since it's already a day later.

I go back to work. I'm fed right up. For the millionth time this month, I'm wondering if it's time to get a real job.

Of course, now Sam has no money because Max had to spend it all forgetting his experience. So actually, neither of them has any money, and Sam hits me up for fifty bucks. This is part of his routine. When Sam has money he has to hurry up and blow it so he can start borrowing from friends. That way he'll owe most of what he makes on his next trip out, and that will take care of his next month or so of desperation. He needs to know there's a definite span of worry time ahead the way normal people need to know they have the rent ahead.

When he's close to down and out—I mean when he literally hasn't eaten for a couple of days—he gets a look of grim satisfaction on his face and starts telling people that the jig is up. He'll come into the bar and I'll say, "Sam, what's happening?" and he'll say, "Gabe, the jig is up." I can say anything to him. I can ask him about his car, women, his folks, work, and all he'll say is the jig is up. Then he'll tell me he hasn't eaten for a week and hit me up for a ham and cheese. It's like he's warming up to die of starvation, but can never quite commit.

("Ah *Gabe*," says Kris. "The little *raspberries*. We have to make the *allowance*.")

I give him the fifty bucks. To be fair, I generally have a Sam-stash behind the bar. Every time he gets off the boats, he tosses me a couple of hundreds and doesn't say a word. He pretends it's a present, like I should go buy something nice with it, but really it's an advance on what he'll be owing me by the time he goes out again.

I guess I shouldn't complain. No one makes me laugh like Sam. And he does treat me to excellent dinners when he's flush. He loves to dress up and go out. He'll call me from Powell River or wherever he's docked and tell me he's on his way home and I should make a reservation at some fancy restaurant. After dinner we'll go back to his place and listen to music (if he has chairs—I refuse to sit on that foamy).

The flowers are a nice touch too. Every once in a while, he wanders into the bar and tosses me a dozen pink roses. He knows I like the pink ones. Last month he outdid himself. He and Dutch wandered in after the lunch rush carrying a long wooden box with two pink roses taped to the top. It looked like a small coffin, and they were so straight-faced, I thought for an awful moment that Dutch's dog Frances had died. But as they were hoisting it onto the bar, Sam said, "We thought we'd buy you a little drink, Gabe."

Turns out there was a huge bottle of champagne in the box. It was called a methuselah. Pretty cute, I have to admit—but not in a sticky way.

I remind Sam that he promised months ago to change the

address on his driver's license. He looks surprised. "But Gabe, I *did*," he says. I'm *sure* I did. *Didn't* I?"

I refuse to get started. I go back to pulling pints with fresh resolve: Tomorrow I'll do nothing but write for five solid hours before I go to work. I think I'll make the main character a therapist. Her ex will be something arty—an architect, maybe, or a filmmaker. I haven't decided who the sticky one will be—maybe both, in different ways—but I think a professional atmosphere will elevate the theme. They say you should write about what you know, but there have to be limits. If I stuck to the rules, my work would be full of Maxes and Sams. I'd never get down to any real writing.

I repeat my resolve. Five solid hours without fail. And this time I'll ignore the door, even if they send out the army.

* * *

Meanwhile, just to tidy up:

As it turned out, Max did have to do a little time for all the trouble he caused—eventually. He also had to pay Mike's lawyer fees. Sam was off the hook a week later when Mike arranged a meeting with him and the two Safeway cops, who of course could not identify him. So car theft was added to the list of misdemeanours.

All would have gone well with Max, who was giggling for the next month about his getaway, if it weren't for an incident at Harvey G. Hawes.

Harvey's is the next-to-last pub going west on Fourth Avenue, Crawley's being the last. Max had been barred from Harvey's for six months and his term was up, so it was time for him to go back and mark the occasion by drinking too much, trying to steal something and getting barred again. It's Max's way of making a statement. Harvey's is not his pub, and he likes people to know it. He has no respect for the place because it's kind of fancy compared to Crawley's, and according to Max, it has no heart.

So it was Max's biannual barring from Harvey's, and all would have gone according to plan—that is, Max would have accepted being barred, gone quietly and shown up at Crawley's with the latest version of his story—if it weren't for the fact that Harvey's had recently hired a new bartender. He was a nervous young fellow who had only been on the job a few days, so when Max started tearing into the place and out-loudly wondering what to steal, the young fellow panicked. As luck would have it, the night manager was up at Jiminy's on his dinner break and there was no one on the door, so he was alone at the bar. He didn't yet know the regulars, so he didn't feel he could ask for help. Besides, he didn't know if they'd be for or against him, since they were all just taking in the show like it was routine. Which of course it was.

So he called the cops. He acted like nothing was happening, didn't even give Max a heads-up. Just called the cops and waited. And who should show up to take him away? The two cops from the Safeway parking lot. Max says the look on their faces was almost worth it. He says it was just like the look on Gray Rateller's face when he found an extra three grams of powder under his kitchen table.

Never a man to rail against fate, he claimed he needed a few months to dry out anyway. To the cops, he reportedly said, "You got me," pounded his last half-pint and went quietly.

Sam says it was the greatest moment of poetic justice ever known to Vancouver. He's taking me to West's on Friday to celebrate. Five-course dinner, different wine with every course, all in Max's honour. He'll visit Max on Sunday and tell him all about it. He says Max appreciates an expensive gesture.

We'll probably go back to Sam's after dinner and listen to music—if there's anything to sit on besides the foamy, that is. I will *not* sit on that foamy.

DUTCH THE GREEK

DUTCH THE GREEK

Vigorous debates are not uncommon in bars, and they sometimes go on for days. They can be volatile, entertaining, and occasionally enlightening—if the debaters have civil tongues and reasonably sound positions.

The Great Debate over the ethics of Dutch the Greek is by far the most heated and longstanding war-of-the-words in the history of Crawley's. It began on a Thursday some months ago in the section I happened to be serving and it has continued in that section every Thursday since.

Because the section requires a level of attention that goes above and beyond the usual call, none of my co-workers have wanted to serve it. So I've been the designated server from the get-go. I agreed to this initially to avoid bickering, but later because I found the entertainment value to be worth the added effort.

With one caveat:

Since the attendance and identities of the debaters vary considerably from week to week and mine do not, I have inadvertently become the constant in a diverse and ever-expanding sea of variables. This in itself is not a problem. However, with it has come the laughable assumption that along with taking orders and serving beer at warp-speed, I am also keeping track of every key point that has been raised, ratified, defeated, or dismissed.

I admit that I'm partly to blame for the added challenge because I started calling people out early in the debate for recycling points that had already been defeated—or worse, that defied logical discourse altogether. I couldn't help it; I was there. As it became more evident that I was keeping track, if only for the sake of my own sanity, the assumption grew that I would continue.

Most of the time, all this means is that when the volume or logic gets too ridiculous, heads turn my way and I'm expected to make a pronouncement. Which will most often take the form of a nod, a headshake, or a rolling of the eyes.

I should probably add that I meet the challenge of tracking propositions with a somewhat slapdash formula for improv logic that may not completely accord with the more stringent regulations of debate protocol. In my own defense: when you work in a busy bar, time is of the essence.

* * *

For those who don't know him, Dutch's real name is Nikolas Van Snijk—pronounced "Sneek." (Seriously. Greek mother, Dutch father.) Because the name lends itself so aptly to the nickname, "Nikky-the-Sneak," and because that nickname is the one area in which Nikky—otherwise a very funny guy—loses his sense of humour entirely, his best friend Sam dubbed him Dutch the Greek. Nikky did not protest, so Dutch it is.

In a nutshell, the debate concerns the "procurement" by Dutch of a logging skidder for Johnny (Rotten) Roxford.

To understand why Dutch felt compelled to gift Johnny with such a large and expensive piece of equipment, it is helpful to know that Johnny had been suffering from a deep and abiding depression—a premature mid-life crisis, really—due to being evicted from his own pub on Vancouver Island.

Johnny had spent years planning and building his pub. It had taken huge amounts of money and work, and a few political favours. The problem was, when he was not completely immersed in hard work, he was a wild man. He drank too much, got far too loud, and said rude things to women.

Once the heavy lifting was over and the bar was up and running, Johnny had less to do. Predictably, he became more and more feral. When his wife finally threw up her hands and walked out, he fell into a steep, noisy decline. After being kicked out of his bar one too many times by his best friend and doorman, Frank, and after neglecting to pay his mortgage far too many times, the bank foreclosed and Johnny was out.

Like the rest of us, Dutch was fond of Johnny and wanted to see him climb out of his hole. Unlike the rest of us, Dutch found a way to do it.

Johnny had run off to the north end of Vancouver Island to work for a logging outfit. He'd logged when he was younger and he knew the ropes. After a short time on the job, his entrepreneurial spirit kicked back in and he applied for a hand-logging tenure on a small section of Crown land. When the tenure was granted, he perked right up.

There was only one problem: Though he had the skills and a truck, Johnny did not have a skidder. Nor did he have the money or credit to buy one.

Dutch knew Johnny was strapped. He also knew where there were skidders to be had, and he happened to have a talent for operating heavy machinery.

A little background:

Dutch had run away from his Ontario home when he was fifteen and taken a job driving a tractor on a farm in South

Carolina. He was a big guy even then and looked older than his years. He claims he rolled his first tractor in the first hour of his first day on the job. Left it lying on its side in the middle of a field with the motor running and ran away. Not knowing what to do next, he continued taking jobs driving tractors and running away till he got the hang of it. At some point, when he had a little money, he took a course and branched out. He now works on towboats, which is how he met Sam. Both Sam and Dutch have been regulars at Crawley's for years.

Continuing on:

Everyone knew Dutch was confident with big rigs. As chance would have it, he was also familiar with the Bison Tractor lot in Vancouver. He'd worked there for a short while, loading and unloading semis and shuffling them around.

At 6:00 a.m. one morning, he strolled onto the Bison lot as if he was coming to work. He walked casually over to an eighteen-wheeler that happened to be carrying a skidder and climbed into the driver's seat. The keys for semis are often left in the ignition during the day—no one worries about theft that huge in daylight—and this was no exception. He turned the key, gave the engine a moment to warm and drove off the lot.

From Bison's, he went straight to Horseshoe Bay, where he boarded the 8:00 a.m. ferry for Nanaimo. By 10:20, he was driving north on the Island Highway. He continued north for about five hours, reaching Johnny's turn-off by midafternoon.

Johnny greeted him with a toke and a bear hug. Before getting into anything serious, they unloaded the skidder and turned the semi around. Then they broke out the Scotch.

Though his cabin was rough and his kitchen modest—two propane burners—Johnny knew that Dutch loved his food. He prepared what Dutch called a "memorable" steak dinner and they spent a pleasant evening catching up.

At 10:00 a.m. the next day, Dutch left Johnny's and drove the much lighter eighteen-wheeler back down-island. ("A little tricky on the curves," he said. "Kept thinking I still had a load...") About halfway to Nanaimo, he pulled in to a rest stop, parked the rig and ambled away. He walked down the highway for about twenty minutes, then thumbed a ride to Parksville, where he caught a bus to Nanaimo. He arrived in time for the 4:00 p.m. ferry to Vancouver and was back in time to tell Sam all about it over dinner.

No one knows exactly how Bison got their semi back, but someone from the Island would have called it in, and someone from Bison's would have gone to pick it up. By all accounts, it was not at the rest stop for long. Johnny's life gained new traction—quite literally—and with much hard work, his sanity and solvency were restored.

* * *

The debate began as the story of Dutch's "grand gesture" slowly trickled in to Crawley's. No one talked about it openly, of course—at least, not at first. But as the oblique references became more frequent and less oblique, more heads would nod knowingly.

Someone might bring up the challenges of reversing a semi, for example. Which might lead to a discussion of heavy-duty equipment. The topic of logging might come up, then logging machinery and skidders. Inevitably, someone would remember they'd heard about a theft at Bison's.

Names might be dropped along the way (*Anyone seen Dutch lately?* Or *How's Johnny Rotten doing—still on the Island?*), but never, of course, when Dutch was present.

It wasn't until Jack Clements and Mike Styles heard the story that anyone thought to question the ethics of the thing. Out loud, that is. Jack, a high school English teacher, expressed shock and indignation right off the bat. Not so much at the theft itself as the fact that nobody else was expressing shock and indignation.

"What—so you all just believe in helping yourselves now? You think this is democracy?"

Mike, a criminal lawyer, was more concerned about consequences:

"Jesus, you guys! This is not some little high school prank! It's theft over $5000! That's grand larceny—an indictable offence! Don't you dare come running to me when the poop hits the fan—I know nothing about this!"

Hoping to settle them both down, Sam announced in a case-closed voice that the gesture was 100% justified:

"Jack, Mike—it saved Johnny's bacon and rescued him from depression... And possibly destitution... And maybe even alcoholism. (Well, maybe not that, but still)..."

Mike: "But Sam, what he did was illegal!"

Sam: "Sure, but he returned the semi. I mean he did the right thing as much as he could under the circumstances..."

Jack: "Oh for Pete's sake, Sam! What else was he going to do with something as huge as an eighteen-wheeler? Besides, he didn't need it, he couldn't use it and he couldn't have sold it—so he couldn't possibly have profited from it any more than he already had. And leaving it at a rest stop on the highway is not the same as returning it."

Sam: "Maybe not exactly, Jack, but he knew they'd get it back, so it's nearly the same."

Mike: "No, it is not. He made them come and get it. That's a big nuisance for any company. And it's still illegal."

Sam: "Well I say they deserve a big nuisance. They're a big corporation—corrupt by definition. If Johnny hadn't got that skidder, it would've been used to clear-cut some gorgeous old forest that would never again get to grow big trees. Do you really support that level of greed and devastation, Mike? After it's already wrecked all our forests? If you want to talk ethics, you should remember that Johnny's using that skidder for selective hand logging—a practice we should've returned to decades ago. He's turning his one little patch of forest into a nice sustainable habitat. I call that heroic. Really, if you think about it, a stolen skidder is a small price to pay..."

Jack: "Oh for Christ's sake, Sam! We're talking about the ethics of Dutch the Greek here, not some romance Johnny's having with his 'little patch of forest.'"

Sam: "Same thing when you get right down to it, Jack. Remember they were in it together."

Ah, the bar debate. The untamed beauty of it. The sheer genius of the logic-defying leap from apples to oranges.

A few people nod their heads and look down at their beer. A few get up to go to the washroom, never to return. A few look my way. I roll my eyes and start wiping down tables, grateful to be off in an hour.

Professor Wiebel now surprises us all by raising his hand. Wiebel is a quiet, formal man in his mid-eighties who used to teach math at UBC. Mike had him in first year, which is how we know.

The professor always wears a brown suit and tie and frequently gives lectures to an invisible audience. He nods slowly when he lectures, his right hand moving in gentle swoops. He is the only person at Crawley's who ever raises his hand to speak. Because he does so rarely, we all come to attention.

"Now," he says, looking slowly around the tables. "You boys and girls have drifted right off the short end of the slipper."

We all lean in.

"*Parsimony*," he says in a loud whisper. "That's the sticker." After a short, sober pause, he nods and says, "Very well then. Let's see you pull those mittens off!" Then he nods again, as if dismissing a class, and returns to his usual position—right arm on the back of his chair, head back, eyes slowly circling the ceiling.

We lean back out.

"What do you think he means?" someone whispers.

"Stop whispering!" shouts Weibel. "And no more leaping about! Short end of the slipper!"

"He said 'parsimony'—do you think he's referring to Occam's Razor?" someone asks.

"*No!*" shouts Mike, as he puts on his coat. "He's asking for a little effing logic!" He strides out, trying—as many have tried before him—to slam the unslammable door. The door swings gently back.

"Boy, someone sure got up on the wrong side of the bed today," says Sam.

* * *

Over time, for the sake of discretion, the incident of the stolen skidder became known as "the Dutch-capade." To spare the consciences of people like Jack and Mike, who felt compromised knowing too much detail, the debate took on more of a hypothetical tone.

Manny, the baker across the street, might bring it up by saying, "Okay—the question is still on the table: If a person steals an object and gives it to another person to help them out, does their act of kindness justify their crime or not?"

To which Frank, the bike-shop guy next door to Manny, replies, "Manny, you can't just ask if the end justifies the means without knowing a bunch of other things first. Like what the object is, for instance—you need to know how big it is, how expensive it is, what it's used for, where it comes from, and all that. And you need to know if the person who gets it could have got it some other way—like legally, right? And then there's the motive—you need to know what the motive of the giver is. What if he isn't really being kind? Think about it—what if he's just showing off?"

To which Mike the lawyer inevitably declares, "Frank, you're just not getting it—a crime is a crime is a crime! Details are completely irrelevant. Political Science 101: society only works because we have rules we agree to. If we all went around making exceptions of ourselves, we'd have anarchy!"

To which, predictably, a chorus of voices sings "Yeah! Let's hear it for anarchy!" and Mike goes and stands at the bar.

At some point, I start taking notes. As the only one keeping track—and possibly the only one who cares—I'm frequently having to call out new debaters for introducing old points. Of which there are many. I'm also having to call out regular debaters for trying to make old points look like new ones. I am now using my words:

"Old point, new paint, John. Still doesn't fly."

"Defeated twice last week, Geena."

"Dismissed for lack of logic, Fred. Five times already. Try to keep up, people."

Overall, the most compelling argument for the right-leaning debaters is Mike's: Theft is illegal; we can't just break the law for any old friend; if we did, society would fall apart. This argument consumes a great deal of time and takes many different shapes, mainly in the form of "what-ifs":

"What if it was *your* skidder, innocently parked in *your* backyard, and someone came along and drove it away?"—Or—"What if it was your *uncle's* skidder, that he was using every day, and someone came along and drove it away?"

To which someone could be counted on to reply, "Yeah, but *which* uncle, right? That's the issue. If it was Uncle Jack's skidder, I'd shoot the guy. No way would that be okay. Uncle Jack is a sweetheart. But if was Uncle Herb's skidder, hey, take it away! That guy is such a dirt-bag. Did I tell you what he said when I got laid off last Christmas...?"

The most compelling argument for the left-leaners is Sam's: Society *is* the problem, and it *needs* to fall apart; ergo, the stolen skidder is an agent of positive change. Various Robin Hood scenarios are introduced to "prove" that stealing from the rich to give to the poor could actually strengthen society because it would boost the economy: More people would have the means to buy more stuff, pay more taxes, etc.

To which one of the more academically-minded (usually poor Mike) will say, "Wait a minute—you can't have it both ways, you guys! You can't claim that a crime is justified because it's helping society fall apart and then try to advance your claim by saying the same crime will make society stronger. That's a total contradiction! It's like saying we should rebel against the status quo in order to reinforce the status quo! Read your Bateson, for Christ's sake!"

To which I will say, "Mike's right, you guys. No switch-hitting," and resolve to read my Bateson.

There are many other arguments, all with many permutations, and to quote the professor, they all drift far from "the short end of the slipper."

So when Boris (Beets) Niles chimes in with a point that is genuinely new, I'm delighted. And grateful.

Beets is Crawley's designated poet, a position he has held for about four years. His original nickname was "Beethoven," but it got shortened to "Beets" when he dyed his Mohawk purple.

A point of general interest: There may or may not be one poet in a neighbourhood bar, but there will generally not be two. This is because bar poets tend to be troubled. One is just containable; two would overwhelm the bar's emotional capacity.

Who gets to be the designated poet depends almost entirely on who gets there first. Once the terrain has been claimed, late arrivals generally don't stand a chance. It's a "fruity niche," as the Brits might say, and one that's not readily relinquished.

Beets, like most troubled poets, is an accomplished sufferer. I think the debate actually gave him a much-needed break. The overt cause of his suffering is Kristina—a fellow server at Crawley's and a very wise woman who will not let Beets sleep with her. Sadly, Beets does not move on. It's not in his nature.

Back to the debate:

Through most of the discussion, Beets had stayed parked at his usual table against the wall, writing longhand in his usual yellow notepad. As the debate wore on, he'd look up from time to time, cock a bored ear and get back to work.

On the night in question, he actually got up and wandered over to the debating section, where he hovered for a while with the other onlookers. The anarchy question had come up again, and Brad Bilker, another towboat guy, was covering the usual ground:

"The thing to remember about anarchy is that it's already with us: Disaster Capitalism, my friends, by any other name. It's just so huge and global and embedded that we've stopped seeing it. But we all know it's running the show. What else would you call something that's ruining the habitats of every life on the planet, including its own? (Well, except maybe the viruses.) If that's not anarchy, I don't know what is. You know how the dictionary defines anarchy? Don't guess, I looked it up: It's "a state of disorder that's due to the absence or non-recognition of authority." Welcome to the world we live in! No legitimate authority—unless you concede that Greed rules—and no recognition of the one authority our survival actually depends on: Mother Nature."

Jacob, the jeweller at the end of the block, is nodding. "Brad's right. No other animal on the planet puts a slow-release time bomb in their own backyard and then hangs around waiting for the fireworks. It's completely perverse."

The conversation wends its way back to the subject of someone stealing something that gives someone else the power to do some good. Which somehow leads to a lively discussion about small-scale versus large-scale violations and whether or not scale should count when it comes to consequences.

Manny is on the "not" side: "So according to Mike, all I get is a slap on the wrist for a theft of $4999. But for a theft of $5000—one dollar more—I go to jail. I mean it doesn't seem fair."

Jeremy Dangelieu is now clamouring to speak, so everyone takes a breath. Jeremy needs about a ten-second run at it to get his words out. He makes a revving sound as he's warming up:

"Rrrrrrr, ruh-ruh-ruh. Rrrrrrrrr (etc.) So why not just tell them it was on sale, Brad?"

Brad: "What?"

Jeremy: "The thing you stole that cost $5000. Just tell them it was on for half-price, right? That way it's only worth $2500, you see what I'm saying? You'll be way under the limit."

Brad: "They wouldn't believe me, Jeremy."

Jeremy: "Your word against theirs, Brad."

Brad nods: "Good point, Jeremy. I'll tell them it was on sale."

Jeremy beams and we all give him a nod. You can tell he's feeling pretty good about helping Brad out, and no one wants to spoil his moment. But it's hard to move the discussion along from here. The topic of scale peters out and the debaters start looking restless.

Then Beets steps up: "You know, this debate has been going on for weeks, and none of you—not one person—has ever brought up the poetry of the thing. Are you all just a bunch of philistines? Have you never actually pictured the heist itself? (I mean the Dutch-capade—sorry.) Can you not see the guy sauntering onto that lot and climbing into that semi like he owns it? And then starting it up and driving it off the lot, cool as cool, when he probably hasn't driven one for years? And then taking it all the way to the top of the Island and back in twenty-four hours? It's beautiful! It's a fucking real-life adventure! AND IT DIDN'T HAPPEN ON A FUCKING SCREEN!!!"

For the first time in the history of Crawley's, the bar has a moment. One of the Aussies claps his hands three times from the stand-up bar. Even the unflappable Kristina looks up from serving a table and smiles. People are nodding thoughtfully, and for one remarkable moment, no one has a word to say.

The debate takes an interesting turn from here. It still swivels around whether a good end justifies an illegal means, but it branches out. Poetry as an end has now entered the equation. As a justification for illegal means, it brings up new questions.

Jacob: "Wait a minute here. What if it turns out to be bad poetry? Like if a certain person botches a certain heist and gets caught, and another person is still short a skidder, would we still say the means justifies the end?"

Mannie: "But who says a botched heist is necessarily bad poetry, Jacob? Maybe it's just a different kind of poetry. Like darker, but still full of danger and excitement, right? You don't call it bad poetry just because someone strikes out in the first inning..."

Sam: "We're not talking baseball here, Mannie."

Beets: "Sure we are, Sam. Everything is poetry if you look at it right."

Sam: "What, you're saying my shoe is poetry?"

Beets: "Absolutely. If you look at it right."

Sam goes to the washroom.

The debate now goes a little sideways as a new discussion starts up around what you can call poetry and whether or not there's any way to tell the good from the bad. When Beets insists that it's entirely subjective, the debaters look uneasy. The implication is that any kind of poetic objective could be seen to justify any kind of questionable means.

People start wondering where it's all going to end. If even a shoe can be poetry (if you look at it right), then all anyone has to say to get off the hook is that they did it for the poetry. And if no one can claim to know the difference between the good and the bad, it could be rotten poetry at that.

No one but Beets is happy with this. People start looking vaguely around and the usual heads swivel in my direction. I'm about to raise an eyebrow when I notice Professor Weibel has his hand up. I nod in his direction and we all turn.

Weibel looks slowly around the tables and leans in. When he's satisfied that he has our attention, he shouts, "Slice up the pie, you ninnies! Slice up the muddy pie! All pie and no slices leaves Jack in the bottle! Class dismissed for absence of ship-members! And sprinkle on those modulators, for God's sake! Liberal sprinkles! Ha! Words belong to everyone!"

Then, rather uncharacteristically, he says "*Sheesh!*" and settles back into his chair.

"What pie?" says Jeremy.

"The *poetry* pie," says Mike, with a withering look. As usual, he is in attendance but wishing he were anywhere else. "He's saying we have to break it down. Poetry is too broad a class to work with. Especially if certain people insist that everything is poetry. You can't go anywhere with that. You have to slice up the pie. Decide what kind of poetry you're talking about—if any—and then break it down further. Like if it's a sonnet or an ode, is it tragic or romantic or what? And if it's romantic, is it elegant or cheesy or what? Those are the 'modulators.'"

"Ah," says Brad. "The *modifiers.*"

"Sprinkled on," says Jeremy.

"Yes," says Mike. "Liberally. Which should make it harder for certain people to bandy words about however they like. As in calling everything that happens poetry."

Beets is now scowling.

"Hang on," says Brad. "The Dutch-capade isn't a sonnet or an ode or any of those kinds of poetry."

"Of course it isn't," says Beets, half-rising in agony. "It isn't *written* poetry. Neither is sex, or a smile, or a shoe. But you can still call them poetry. The trouble with some people is they think everything that's a little illegal is a crime and nothing but. But then, some people wouldn't know poetry if they fell into a vat of it."

Things are heating up now and the debaters are starting to frown. Eyes are roving, phones are being checked, escapes being plotted.

***

As it turns out, no one needs to plot any further because Sam now wanders back to the debating section. And to everyone's surprise, he has Dutch in tow. They are both grinning broadly.

It's a strikingly nervous moment. The debaters get all chatty and fidgety and find interesting things to look at on the other side of the room.

The thing is, everyone knows without quite knowing it that Dutch has been tracking the debate from the get-go through Sam. Who stays up-to-date through me. But of course, no one ever mentions it when Dutch is present because no one is supposed to know anything about it.

Dutch comes up to the main table and says hello. Then he gets right to it:

"Of course I did it for the poetry, you jam-tarts. And the poetry was excellent, if I do say so myself. It was a great adventure that didn't happen on a screen (thank you Beets) and nobody got hurt. Hey, we make up the words. When we call something poetry, we all know what we mean."

Jeremy is now revving like mad.

"*Rrrrrr-ruh-ruh-ruh-rrrrrrrrr, etc...* Adventure-Poetry, Dutch! Do you see what I'm saying? If you slice up the pie? It was like an adventure and it was like poetry! So—'Adventure-Poetry!' And then you need to sprinkle on the modulators—like it was 'excellent' and it was 'live,' right? So you get 'Excellent Live Adventure-Poetry!' That's a slice right there!"

"Right on, Jeremy," says Dutch. "It's a perfect slice. Fucking 'Excellent Live Adventure-Poetry.'"

"The best kind," says Beets. "If you look at it right."

* * *

At that, everyone settles back, and we all somehow know the debate is over. Not resolved with anything resembling logic, of course, but finished with a nice flourish. "Excellent Live Adventure-Poetry" just sounds tasty.

"Words belong to everyone," says Jeremy, and everyone gives him a nod.

THE DEVIL SPINNERS

THE DEVIL SPINNERS

Haley's back in town. I saw him today, in front of the old Virgin Records store on Robson and Burrard. It must be eight months since I saw him last, maybe even nine. I remember it was late summer, and a super-hot afternoon.

I tend bar at Crawley's—officially The Crow's Gate Pub—down on West Fourth Avenue. When Haley's in town, he usually comes in around 3:00 p.m., and you always hear him before you see him. "All you need is love!" he'll boom as he walks in the door. He'll come straight to the bar, shouting out greetings to the regulars, and then he'll yell, "A pint of the Pale, Gabe!" even though I'm standing right in front of him.

I remember there were only two other people standing at the bar that day last summer, and the tables were half empty. But still he sounded like he was shouting over an eight-lane freeway at rush hour.

Haley's boom is not aggressive, though. There are people who talk loudly and fill the place up to make themselves important, but with Haley it's something else. Haley definitely fills the place up, but it's not like he's after attention. He's a good-looking guy, about five-eleven and well built. Regular features, thick mass of curly brown hair and a great sideways grin. So he's not exactly starved for attention, especially from the ladies. It's more like he's trying to out-shout his own background roar. Even when he tones it down, he sounds like he's shouting over heavy traffic.

I think he's spent too much time on the road. He's always on his way somewhere or just back from not quite getting there. And it never makes any logical sense. Last year, for instance, he was on his way to Maine for three trips running. He had a friend in Maine who wanted him to come out and help refit a sailboat. Then they were supposed to sail down to Florida and maybe even the Caribbean and charter it out to the tourists. His friend even had the money to do it.

But three times running he showed up back in Vancouver, and when I asked what happened to Maine, he said he nearly got there, but he lost a week in Halifax and never made it. Or Edmonton, or Sudbury, or some other town where he liked the beer.

Haley's a drinker. I mean an all-day, all-night, all-the-time drinker. He drinks slowly and steadily, and I guess I'd never actually seen him sober till today. He's a quiet drinker, in spite of the boom, and he never gets sloppy. The only way you can tell he's had too much is when he closes one eye and squints to get you in focus. That and the way his sentences sometimes stop in mid-air.

I especially remember that afternoon last summer because it was the first time I ever had a real conversation with Haley. I mean a personal one, where something got said. The way it usually goes is I'll say, "Haley! Where've you been?" as he walks in the door, and he'll shout out the names of a few towns. He might add a couple of details about which ones had the best music, but that's about the extent of it.

When he came in that afternoon last summer, I called out, "Haley!" as usual, and asked him where he'd been. He called back, "Gabe! I never got there! I've only nearly-been! I was headed for Maine again, but I got stuck in Halifax!" When I asked where he was headed next, he said he was thinking of making another try for Maine.

"So why didn't you just head out from Halifax?" I asked, "instead of coming all the way back to Vancouver?" He said, "Yeah, I should've. I should've done that, but I like coming back to Vancouver. I like a fresh start. Besides, I'm thinking of swinging down to Portland for a week or two before I leave."

When he swings down to Portland, it's usually for a gig in a bar or club. Haley's a street musician mostly—sings his own songs and plays guitar—but now and then he has a booking indoors. He works the liquor store on Fourth and Alma when he's in Vancouver, which is why he drinks at Crawley's.

Most of the time the conversation just circles around his travels, but that day last summer was different. When Haley came in, there were only two people standing at the bar—George and Tommy Hutchinson—and the place was half empty. George and Tommy are out-of-work carpenters who usually hit the bar around 2:00 p.m. to get away from their wives, and then get called home around 6:00 for supper. They bicker a lot, I think the heat makes them cranky, and people tend to leave them alone.

Haley gets his beer and moves to the other end of the bar, still booming out greetings. There's only a handful of people limply sipping beer in the corners, and their faces are starting to look dented, so I finally have to yell at him to lower the boom. He gives me a nod and tones it down to a whispered shout.

I swing down to the other end of the bar with a couple of pints for Tommy and George, who are drooped across the counter on their elbows, looking cross. As I'm wiping down bottles, they start in. I roll my eyes at Haley, and he gives me a wink. You can't help but listen when George and Tommy get going. You don't want to, but you can't help it.

"Have you checked out that fly, Tommy?" says George.

"What fly is that, George?" says Tommy.

"That fly right in front of your face, Tommy."

"No George, I have not checked out that fly. I did not realize that fly was there, as a matter of fact."

"Well, it is. You should check it out. You ever watched a fly before, Tommy?"

"George, I've seen flies. I've seen probably a dozen million flies in my time. I don't like 'em. Dirty little insects. Carry disease."

"I know you've *seen* 'em, Tommy. I'm asking if you ever *watched* one?"

"Sure I watched 'em. They're boring, George. Flies don't do it for me, okay?"

"It's not the point, Tommy. I'm asking did you ever watch one and you're saying sure, but I don't believe you. Tell me something. What do you hate worse, moths or flies? I bet you hate moths worse, right?"

"I hate 'em both, George—what's the point? Would you mind please telling me what's the point here? I didn't even notice that fly, but now you've pointed it out, that fly's beginning to drive me crazy."

"Ha! That's the point right there," says George. "You see, most times we think it's just moths drive us crazy, they're so blind and stupid, batting away at the light. You want to whack the little suckers. But flies, Tommy, flies can be way worse. Check out that fly. That fly is stuck. That fly has been flying in a holding pattern for the last five minutes. In straight little lines—back, forth, left, right, zig, zag—like a bloody soldier. No ups, no downs, exactly the same height off the bar. That fly has been marching *nowhere* for five minutes. And you know what? It's depressing. You know why? Because it looks like it's going somewhere, that's why. And not only that, it looks like it knows where it's going. And it's going there with *enthusiasm*. But it only lasts a foot, and then it turns around and goes the other way. Depressing. You see, moths are just crazy, Tommy—you can accept that. But flies are another story. Flies are not only crazy, they *think* they know where they're going."

"George, number one, flies can't think. And number two, who cares? I mean so what? Is there a point here? Would you mind please telling me what the point is?"

"*Tchah!*" says George. "You know your problem, Tommy? You ain't interested in life. You think everything's gotta have some fancy point to it."

"No, George, the point is I ain't interested in flies. Especially this one here that's driving me crazy. Now you're welcome to stand here and watch this fly just as long as you like, but I'm going to grab a table and take a load off before the place fills up."

Tommy wanders over to a table against the wall and George stands at the bar watching the fly. Pretty soon he starts looking restless, and after a minute or two he goes and sits down with Tommy.

I'm in that mid-afternoon stupor that happens between 3:00 and 4:00 o'clock—the lull between storms, when there's not enough happening to keep you busy, but just enough to keep you from reading a book. It's the major time warp of the day.

Haley moves closer and without really meaning to, we both start watching the fly. It's zigzagging back and forth inside a precise square of two-dimensional space—about a foot long by a foot wide—and it's staying exactly two feet above the bar. There really is something crazy-making about the way it stops, turns on a dime and pushes off again with such gusto. Like it may have had a few false starts, but this time it really knows where it's going.

We watch for a minute, mesmerized. Then just as I'm thinking it's time for the swatter, it shoots straight up and loops its way over to the exit.

Haley nods approvingly. "GPS reset," he announces. "Must have been losing his bearings with that little routine."

"You mean *finding* his bearings, don't you?"

"No, not necessarily. I mean, sometimes you have to lose them to find them, right? Like when you're fixing to set a new course, but you need a bit of a kick-start."

I shake my head. "Speaking of setting courses," I say, "Are you serious about heading to Maine again?"

He says yes, but for different reasons. Apparently the boat is finished now and his friend has already headed south.

"I'm supposed to join him in Florida," he says. "Mid-September. He wants me to join him in Miami and sail to the Bahamas. But I don't know; I might go back to Wakeville first."

I ask him where Wakeville is and he tells me it's somewhere in the east. He can't say exactly, but it's on the way to Maine. I ask him what's special about it and he gets a cloudy look on his face.

"Well," he says, "That's a story, Gabe. That's a whole story all by itself." Then he clams right up and drifts into space. I get the feeling he's planning his next trip—you can almost see the highways in his eyes.

The place begins to fill around 4:00 and my focus shifts to pouring drinks. At some point I notice Haley is sitting by himself at a table by the door, which is unusual. Most days he strolls around and mixes with the regulars when the place starts filling up.

* * *

I get off at 6:00 and find Haley waiting for me outside. He's got two hours to kill before he's on at the liquor store—someone else has the spot till 8:00—so we decide to go to Joe's next door for supper. He's still got that cloudy look on his face and I ask him what's up.

"Just hungry," he says, so I tell him to order the ribs. They're always huge.

"Not that kind of hungry, Gabe," he says. "I'm way hungrier than that. I could eat a highway right now. I could eat the 101 all the way down to San Francisco. I could eat every truck stop and billboard from here to Halifax."

Then he tries to laugh it off, but his laugh is dry and his lips are stretched too wide across his teeth. He's also jiggling his knee against the table so fast that I'm getting indigestion before I've even looked at the menu.

"Haley," I say, "would you please settle down. You're making me twitchy. You've been eating too many highways already, my friend. I can see every truck stop and billboard you've ever put away, right there on your face. Those highways are eating you, Haley."

"Sometimes I take the train, Gabe," he says. Like that makes a difference. "I caught a freight all the way from Vancouver to Toronto last trip."

I give up and ask him where he got stuck last time.

"Well Gabe, that's a story. Like I said before, that's a whole story all by itself. A funny thing happened on the way to Maine. Watching that fly earlier made me think of it. Made me think of that little town I stumbled on called Wakeville. You might say I lost my bearings in that little town. But some might argue that I found them too. Hard to say, really."

Now from here on the story belongs to Haley. All I've done is write it down as closely as I can remember, and if no one believes it I've got nothing to say. Except maybe to ask why he'd bother to make it up.

HALEY'S STORY

I was in northern New England, heading south. I'd been riding with a trucker since nine in the morning—talkative Republican type—and I'd had about all I could take of *our-man-may-have-his-faults-but*... It's already noon and I haven't had my first beer yet, so I ask him to drop me off at the nearest town. He puts me down by a turnoff in the middle of a big stretch of farmland and tells me there's a town about a mile down the road.

Turns out to be more like three or four miles down the road, but I get a ride about halfway along with an old farmer in a pickup. A really friendly guy named Noah Jay. He's a classic Santa Claus type—white hair, white beard, rosy cheeks, the works.

He looks excited when he sees my pack and guitar and asks me right away if I'm a hobo. "I mean a real one," he says. He wants to know if I travel across the country and ride the rails and go south for the winter and all that. It cracks me up that he's excited about meeting a hobo, so I ham it up a little. After all, I am headed south and I did hop a freight as far as Quebec.

He asks me a bunch of questions about places I've been, and then he tells me he's got a farm on the edge of town and I should drop by for supper if I'm passing that way. And he has this funny tic. He leans in close and blinks a few times when he looks at you, like he's trying to see you better. But he's not a twitchy guy at all. And he's not senile either. He's dandy behind the wheel—keeps his speed up, good reflexes, even though he tells me he's pushing ninety.

After about ten minutes, we pass a big hand-painted Welcome to Wakeville sign, and the farms make way for the first few houses and stores. Noah drives me all the way downtown and drops me on Main Street. He leaves me with careful directions to his place in case I should want a meal or a bed for the night. Gives me a nice feeling.

As we're saying goodbye, he leans in and blinks again. Then it sounds to me like he calls out, "Wakey-wakey!" as he's driving off. I figure he must be a little mixed up after all, but I later discover it's a common expression in the town. Every place you go to has its quirks.

By now it's about 1:00 in the afternoon. I decide to wander the streets a bit, locate the bars and cafes, see if there's a backstreet bar that looks better than the one on Main Street. Turns out the one on Main Street is the only bar in town.

I pass the usual rows of houses with front lawns and cherry trees. They all look well cared for—fresh paint, green grass, a picture-postcard town. But I notice one funny detail: every house I pass has a picture of a rising sun on it.

Now I don't know if I ever mentioned this, but my real name is Helius, which is Latin for "sun." It's supposed to be pronounced "Hay-li-yoos," but people kept calling me "Heely" so I changed it to Haley. Anyway, I've got a thing for suns, and I'm suddenly seeing them everywhere. The town is so solid and straight-looking that they really stick out. Then I remember the wakey-wakey business, and I wonder if it's some kind of play on the town's name—a way to make old Wakeville special, like they do in some of those small-time theme towns.

Anyway, the people seem friendly enough, and there's lots of them around. They smile as they pass, and the kids giggle and look back at you the way kids do. Nobody looks like they're in a big hurry. A friendly town, you can feel it. A little odd, but friendly.

By now it's about 2:00 in the afternoon, and I'm getting hot. I figure the lunch crowd should be gone from the bar, so I head back to Main Street for a cool one.

I like the bar right away. It's at ground level with a row of wood-framed windows that open to the street, just the right height to rest your elbow on. Wooden tables and chairs and a wood floor that's been oiled and swept for about a thousand years and smells like old pencil shavings. Pool table against the far wall, old-fashioned stand-up bar to the left as you walk in. Polished wood and brass, a real beauty.

The bartender's a big friendly guy with curly red hair and freckles. He says howdy and pours me a beer and I settle in at a table by the window.

Across the street is the public library, a long wooden building with big windows all across the front. I can't see inside because the sun's reflecting off the glass, but there's a good view of the street in both directions.

I'm sitting there with my first beer of the day, wondering how far it is to Kittery Point, Maine, where my friend is. I'm trying to decide if I should pull the guitar out now or wait for evening, and I'm wondering if thirty-two dollars will get me to the next one-horse town. I'm also wondering where the next one-horse town is, because the Wakeville part of my map has disappeared into a fold. I'm about to go and ask the bartender when I notice a guy walking by in front of the public library.

He's wearing a black suit jacket, a black tie and no shirt. I mean it's a hot day, but usually you take the jacket off first, right? He's wearing matching black suit pants, about four inches too short, and black shoes with no socks. And he's marching. Back and forth in front of the library, hup-two-three-four, like some kind of one-man military parade.

What's even more surprising is that the people passing him on the sidewalk all seem pretty casual about the guy. But you don't get the feeling they're ignoring him, or pretending he isn't there. The building goes to the end of the street, and lots of times when he gets to the corner, there's people waiting to cross. But nobody looks uncomfortable. Even the mothers with kids give him a nod, like he's no different from anyone else.

I keep watching and realize there's more to the guy's routine than a simple march. When he gets to the end of his route, he does this quick little spin—like a pirouette—and then looks in the library window really fast. Sometimes he jumps the gun and does his spin halfway along, but he always looks in the window right after.

Most of the time he just takes a quick peek, but other times he looks long and hard and leans way in, so his head nearly touches the glass. And he stands there staring with his hands behind his back for maybe five or ten seconds.

If someone comes along and looks in the glass, he stares at them for a moment too—their reflection, I mean—and they stare right back. He gives them a little bow as they walk on by and then he's back on his march, eyes forward, till he reaches the corner. Then he stops, spins, stares, and heads off in the other direction.

For the first while, you get the feeling he doesn't really expect things to turn out. Like when you buy a lottery ticket and you know it's not one of your hot days. You're relaxed about it, but you still have to peek at the numbers.

After a while, though, especially when he starts doing spins in odd places, you can tell he's getting hot. He's throwing himself into the job, you can almost see the sweat flying off him, and he's leaning in before he's even come to a stop. And he's got me staring right along with him. But all I can see is his reflection.

I sit there watching this guy for a good two hours. I mean at first you're looking out of the corner of your eye; you know how it is. Your mind is saying "possible crazy person," and you can't help it, you keep taking little peeks. But two hours later, the guy's still at it, and I'm hypnotized.

Then suddenly, without any warning, he introduces a new move—a little sideline he sneaks in every few trips. He'll be marching along as usual, and then he'll suddenly come to a stop. No pirouette, no staring in the window. He just stops in mid-march. Then he does a slow sidestep, very precise, like he's climbing out of the tub. He lifts one leg up and plants it to the side. Then the other. Then he stands completely still for a while with his legs apart.

After about a minute, he lifts his arms out from his sides really slowly. I mean *slowly.* He gets them even with his shoulders, stops for a moment, then raises them higher, till they make a V above his head. Then he spreads his legs and stands on tiptoe.

He's now spread out like a big X, as high and wide as he can get. I'm waiting for take-off. Well, I'm waiting for *something.* But no. Nothing. He hangs there for maybe three or four minutes, and then he carefully takes himself down. Then he steps back onto the main route and gets on with his march.

Now get this: Every now and then, someone comes along when he's all stretched out like that, and what do you think they do? I mean what would you do? You see a guy hanging all high and wide in the middle of the sidewalk and you're going to give him a wide berth, right? Well, most of them do. Most of them walk on by and stick to business. But now and then, one of them stops for a minute and steps to the side—that same climbing-out-of-the-tub step—and they spread their arms and stretch out right along with him! So now there's two of them hanging there in mid-air!

At first I think they're making fun of the guy. Makes me really uncomfortable to see it. But after two or three times, I can tell they're really into it. They're going slow and getting it right. And they hang there for a couple of minutes, some of them, before they get on their way.

Meanwhile, the guy just goes on with his routine. If someone joins him, it doesn't faze him one bit. Doesn't even look like he notices. He comes out of his spread and gets on with the job, marching and spinning and staring, like that's what he's paid to do.

As I say, by now I'm hooked in. I go up to the bar for my third or fourth beer and ask the bartender if the guy puts in an eight-hour shift or what. He smiles and says, "Some days." Friendly, but not talkative.

At around 4:30, the bar starts to fill and the usual after-work banter starts up. People nod when they catch my eye and I nod back, but I'm still so tuned to the marching man that I'm not really there.

I'm just about to pull out the guitar and bring myself back with a little music when the guy throws a new kink into his routine. Every few trips, when he does his spin, he stares straight across the road, directly into the bar. I can actually feel a kind of "zap" from the man.

My mind's now telling me it's time to get out of here, but I can't quite get in gear. It's like that feeling when your hand goes to sleep and you can't grab hold of anything.

I catch the eye of a man at the next table. He says hello with the same funny blink as Noah Jay, and I ask if he's got something in his eye. He says no, he's just clearing the screen. Turns out this is another local tic.

He shakes my hand and tells me his name is Wyn. "Haley," I say. He nods across the street and asks if I'm enjoying the show. Now I'm embarrassed. I realize they all must think I'm rude, staring at the guy for so long. I don't know what to say, so I shrug like it's no big deal. Like I've seen my share of loonies and this one's nothing special.

"Dougan's something special all right," says Wyn. He looks out the window with a smile. "I caught a *dee*-luxe time-spread from him today. Two, in fact. One on my way to do Johnson's septic, and another one coming back. The man's put in a hard afternoon with all this heat. That's a sticky routine he's doing. He'll be ready for a cold one himself soon."

"I sure as hell would be," says the man beside him. His name is Frank. "You gotta hand it to him, Dougan's no half-miler."

"I caught the spread a few times myself," says another guy. "Have to admit I cheated, though—couple extra loops on the milk run to take me down Main Street one more time. Put the milk run through a time-spread too."

They go on to discuss the finer points of Dougan's routine. Then Wyn says, "Yup, the devil's thrown a shoe today."

I'm starting to wonder where I've landed. Time-spreads and devils throwing shoes are not normal bar talk *anywhere*. I don't care how out of the way a place might be, normal bar talk is football, women and politics.

I want to believe they're just being kind, playing along with the guy so he won't feel left out. Small-town people can be very protective of their loonies. But it's strange that they're playing along with him when he isn't even in the bar.

I ask Wyn quietly if the guy is sick or what.

He looks surprised. "Hell no," he says. "What you're seeing out there is the cure, Haley, not the disease. Our Dougan's a devil spinner. Best in town, if you want the truth. What you're looking at is some heavy-duty preventive maintenance. He's tossing three, maybe four in one pass out there. That takes coordination. What do you think, Frank? Is Dougan tossing three or four today?"

"Three easy," says Frank. "Four if you count the last half hour."

"Tossing what?" I ask. I'm getting a little annoyed.

"Cookies," says Wyn. "If Dougan was at the table right now, he'd say he was tossing cookies."

"Devil-cookies," says Frank. Then he gives me a shot to the arm and they both laugh.

"Hey relax, Haley," says Wyn. "We're just pullin' your leg. Dougan calls 'em cookies because he's the baker here in town. He uses bakery talk for everything. You know, pie-in-the-sky, half-baked notions, that kind of thing. When Dougan talks about devil spinning, he talks about tossing cookies. It's just an expression."

"Yeah," says Frank. "The Dougan method is to make the devil so dizzy he drops his cookie cutter."

"We all have different talk for it," says Wyn. "Dougan says he's tossing cookies. Frank here's a carpenter, so he calls it tossing forms. I work with horses myself, so I like to say the devil's thrown a shoe. It's all the same thing."

So now I'm supposed to be clued in. I'm wondering if there's something funny in the beer. Or if I've been drinking a lot longer than I think.

I ask Wyn what time it is and he says it's 5:00 p.m.—"unless you caught some of Dougan's spread."

Looks like I'm in for a pound. "So what's the deal with the spread?" I ask.

"The time-spread," says Wyn. "You know—we were talking about it before."

I say, "Yeah, I didn't know what it was then either."

"Boy, you really are from out of town, aren't you?" he says. "Time is one of the first shoes you throw when you're... Hey, wait a minute, here comes the man himself. Hold that thought, Haley. We'll take it to the horse's mouth."

"Dougan! Over here!" he calls out.

I look up and see Dougan himself strolling into the bar. He's all chipper and bright-eyed, and everyone looks pleased to see him. A few of the boys go and pat him on the shoulder, and some of them give him a hug.

"Wynnie!" he shouts. "Rise and shine, boy! And while you're at it, find me a chair! Hey Frankie—wakey-wakey!"

Wyn finds him a chair and Frank buys a round of beer. He brings Dougan back to the table and introduces us. Dougan gives me his hand with a howdy and a smile.

He's a big guy, bigger than I thought from across the street, and dark, like maybe he's part Spanish or First Nations. Brown eyes, straight black hair, big white smile. He's built strong and narrow, with wide forearms and oversize hands. A good-looking man, the right side of forty.

He whips out a white T-shirt from his jacket pocket and does a quick change at the table. Then he pulls off the tie and loops it over Wyn's neck. "Free ride, Wynnie—should be a spin or two left in that tie."

Wyn gets up and does a quick spin, then sits back down.

"Speaking of spins," he says, "Haley here hasn't seen a whole lot of cookie-tossing. Fill him in, would you, Dougan? He wants to know what a time-spread is."

"Sure," says Dougan. "That's the part where you step to the side—right or left, doesn't matter. You raise your arms and go into the stretch, then you wait for things to stop. When it's quiet all the way through, the cookie's officially tossed. Time spreads and you spread with it."

He gives me a grin, like Bob's your uncle.

"It's pretty simple," he says, "once you get your focus down. Focus is what counts—that and a good routine. A good routine keeps your certainty level high, and you need that for a cookie toss. Especially if you're tossing time right off the bat."

I tell the man that with all due respect, I don't believe you can get rid of time with some made-up routine. Certainty or no certainty, time is a fact of life.

"True," says Dougan. "But there's time, my friend, and there's *time*. We're just talking about stepping off the line."

"What line?"

"The timeline—that bony little track from Monday to Sunday that rips ahead and pulls apart like a broken zipper. It's the Big Cookie. But it's a simple matter to toss. You just step to the side and make time wide.

I can tell I'm one big squint.

"We all have our time-spreads, Haley, but mostly they happen by accident. Someone close to you dies, or you fall in love when you didn't expect to. Time gets thicker. The moment spreads. When we're tossing time, we're just making it happen on purpose. From there you can toss whatever you like."

"So what else were you tossing?" I ask.

"Mostly me," he says.

Great. I ask how he tosses himself.

"It's a pretty simple routine," he says. "Mainly it's a matter of staring at myself. I use the windows of the library because the reflection's good in the afternoon. I march and spin between stares. You don't usually march without expecting to arrive somewhere, so right away the body has to toss its expectations. Odd clothes help, too.

"The spin is for dizziness. Watching fixed objects flying around in space is a great way to lose your moorings.

"The stare takes a bit of persistence. You keep on staring till you don't see yourself anymore. Like saying a word over and over till all you're left with is rhythm and sound. With the stare, what you're left with is form and colour.

"You start noticing that everything has a pulse to it. If you listen a certain way, the little pulses all join up and you can actually catch a snatch of the Big Tune.

"The main thing is, you've tossed out all the add-ons that make life clunky. You've spun yourself free and clear. Simple mental hygiene, hey Frankie?"

Frank takes an invisible towel and passes it between his ears.

I've had at least six beers by now, and I'm shifting into overload. I deserve to be unconscious. The funny thing is, I'm not feeling drunk. If anything, I'm feeling too sober. It's not a bad feeling exactly, but I'm ready for a change of pace.

At the same time, I'm not quite ready to leave because I want more beer. I pull out my guitar and start fooling around. I keep it low, so I won't interrupt the talk. This feels better. The voices fade out and soon I'm hearing nothing but the music. I notice I'm making new sounds, too, which is odd for me. It feels like I'm chasing a melody—something sweet and sad that's just out of reach.

When I try to nail it down, it disappears. So I keep myself off to the side, hoping the guitar will charm it out. The sound rises and falls and snakes around this way and that. One minute it's all soft and curly, the next it's doing some crazy flamenco-thing.

I should mention that I've never played flamenco in my life. I've never done half the things that guitar was doing that night. To be honest, it's been years since I've been inspired about music at all. You get lazy; you stick to the songs you know, and sooner or later you're sick of them all. You play for the crowd, and you forget the excitement you felt when you were first trying things on. But suddenly, in this weird little town that I can't even find on my map, I'm back on the hook. I'm excited—*excited*, Gabe. Now that's a word I haven't used in years.

What's even more surprising, the people in the bar are getting excited too. Someone turns off the jukebox and they all gather round to listen. And they really listen. It's like they're out there with me on the hunt.

I play for a good hour without stopping. When I finally take a break—when the guitar finally gives me a break—they bring down the house. They're whistling and stomping and calling for more. People are up buying beer for the table and I'm sitting there with a goofy grin on my face, wondering what the hell is up. I feel like I should tell them this is not my usual routine; I have no idea where it's going, or if it's still going. Maybe it's all over, I want to say. Or it isn't *me*. But I can't pin my mind to the thought.

So I don't say anything. I decide if I play some more, great, and if I don't, too bad. Well, no sooner have I decided this than the urge to play comes on again. Only this time I'm not disappearing into the music by myself—I'm taking the whole bar with me. I'm asking people what they want to hear, and they're calling out this and that, and before you know it, I've played three polkas and shifted into bluegrass. With that same shy melody peeking out from every tune.

They clear a space in the middle of the room, and some of the ladies start dancing. Three fiddles appear, then a tambourine, and pretty soon there's half a dozen of us playing on something. At some point, I look up and see old Noah Jay walking in the door. He smiles and waves and pulls out a harmonica. And can he play! Then someone gets spoons from the bar, and the ones who aren't dancing play with those.

Now you'd think with all this confusion of talent, the sound might be a little short in quality. But no. People keep shouting out requests, and it seems like there's nothing we can't do.

If I was ever to rank my high times, I'd have to say that evening was one of the highest. And oddly enough, it didn't end that night. My whole time in Wakeville was like that. Every time I'd think it's got to end soon, I'd get a picture of Dougan's timeline, and instead of looking down it, I'd take a little step to the side. I'd even do it for real sometimes, walking down the street. And I'd think, so what if it ends? I don't have to watch the end coming, do I? What good would that do anyway?

Like I say, it was a memorable night. At around midnight, things wound down and people came by to say goodnight. I must have met half the town that night. Everyone's got a place to stay if I need one, and they all want me to stick around for the big dance that's coming up a week from Saturday. The town's having some kind of anniversary and I tell them I'll be there for sure.

Well this is only Wednesday, and I'm still planning to be in Kittery Point the next week, but I don't see a need to mention it. I figure I'll see how tomorrow shapes up and play it one day at a time. I have a strong suspicion that things will look different in the morning—they usually do after a dozen beers—and I'm not expecting the glow I have on to survive a major hangover.

* * *

I spend the first night at Noah's place. His house is south of town on a long rise, backed by a stretch of pines. You can hear a creek bubbling through the trees as we reach the door.

He fixes me a bed in a small glassed-in sun porch, points out the bathroom and fridge, and tells me to make myself at home. Then he heads upstairs to bed.

Now I hate to admit this, but the first thing I do once I figure Noah's asleep is to sneak into the kitchen and check out his fridge. I should mention that I'm generally a man of impeccable foresight when it comes to potential hangovers. But in all the excitement, I've forgotten to secure myself a six-pack. And I'm more than a little nervous about facing the day without beer.

I open the fridge with my fingers crossed, and I swear I'm

about ready to go and kiss the old man when I see a case of beer inside. A dozen little frosty soldiers, just waiting to come on duty. I figure I can replace them tomorrow, so I take a couple with me to the sun porch.

I expect to be out like a light as soon as my head hits the pillow, but it turns out I'm not sleepy at all. My mind is racing around, playing back the day, and I'm still trying to chase down that tune. I lie around for about an hour, willing myself to pass out.

Now there is nothing worse in my world than being conscious at the start of a hangover. And I know from experience that there is nothing more futile than trying to outrun one, especially by willing myself to pass out. The music is still buzzing around in my head, so I grab my guitar and slip outside, thinking I'll wander off to where I can play without waking Noah.

It's a beautiful starry night, warm and still, with about two-thirds of a moon. I follow the sound of the water till I get to the creek, then walk alongside it till I find a good rock. Then I sit for a while, listening to the sounds.

At some point, I pick up the guitar and plunk away, but nothing much is coming, so I set it down and sit some more.

The truth is, I like to be fairly comatose by this time of night; you probably put that together already. And I can say with some confidence that anyone else who had to spend a whole day in my head would feel the same way. Furthermore, there are worse things than beer for giving a person a break. Not that I'm one to glorify alcohol, but there are worse things.

For some reason, though, this night is different, despite all I've had to drink. It's hard to nail it down exactly, but I feel like I've made it out of some stuffy attic room. The stale, whiney voices in my head have all gone quiet and I'm feeling the warmth of the air on my face. It's mixing with the steamy heat coming up from the ground, and all through the heat is the smell of pines.

The sounds are in focus too, especially from the creek. Instead of hearing one big general water sound, I'm hearing hundreds of little ones, all weaving in and out of each other. I look at the stones on the bottom of the creek and realize that all those different shapes are what's making the sound.

Well, we all know that sounds are made by something passing through something else, but the truth is, I only ever knew it in theory. Now for some reason, it's registering. I'm looking at the creek and seeing a huge long instrument that's tuned by all the angles of the stones.

Now I'm in trouble. I'm realizing there's an infinity of things around me to realize. And I'm feeling behind. So behind I could never catch up in a million years. All of a sudden there's so much to hear that I have to close my eyes and concentrate on one sound at a time, just so I won't go crazy.

There's the wind in the trees, and the little sounds of insects chewing on things. There's an owl hooting somewhere, and animals burrowing, and twigs breaking. And every time I notice a particular sound or smell, it amazes me. For no reason.

I'm sitting there tossing a cookie, Gabe. Damned if I'm not throwing a shoe.

Then there's all the things to *see*. This patch of clover at my feet, for instance, that's gone all dry and summer-brown. It's a stage of clover I usually want to ignore, to be honest. It's depressing. You see a bunch of dried up dead stuff and you want to look at something else, right?

But for some reason, I bend down and pick one of the flowers. I hold it up to the moonlight and see this little brown face with a long hairy beard looking back at me. I find myself saying "Hey, old boy." I'm talking to a *flower*, Gabe. And I get the feeling he's saying "Hey" right back.

Well, at some point, it all starts to feel a bit rich. And I don't know why, but I can tell it's going to make me sad. Something makes me pull away. I find myself climbing back into that musty old attic room and closing the door behind me.

I get back to the house as the first streaks of pink are creeping into the sky. I drink a beer to be on the safe side and climb into bed. This time I'm out like a light.

* * *

I must have logged about four hours when the smell of coffee comes wafting under the door. I'm not usually much of a coffee drinker, but today just the smell of it puts me in the mood.

I know there's a hangover lurking in me somewhere, so I drain the second beer and lie for a while longer. I'm waiting for my head to start pounding, but nothing happens. My bladder wants a little relief, but that's about it.

I begin to wonder if I've stumbled onto the perfect beer. It's a local brew called Nonny's No-Nod, with a picture on the label of that same rising sun. I wonder if it's something extra pure about the water, though I've never really bought all that bull they put in the beer ads.

Still, I'm feeling pretty together for what I've consumed since yesterday. I swing my legs to the floor and test out a partial-vertical. So far so good. I get up and hop around. All good.

The smell of bacon is now mixing in with the coffee, and I realize I'm starving. I pull on my jeans and T-shirt and wander into the kitchen. Noah is manning the skillet and a young girl of about twelve is making toast. They turn and shine identical pairs of bright blue eyes on me, and the girl skips over and shakes my hand.

She tells me her name is Luka-Blue Jay and we're having breakfast outside because it's a good day for clouds. She's already set the table and she thought I'd never wake up.

It turns out Luka is one of Noah's great-grandkids. He has a dozen of them sprinkled around town, and there's usually one or two staying on the farm in the summer.

If Noah looks like Santa, Luka is a female version of Huck Finn. She has straw-blond hair in pigtails down to her waist, a freckled face and an ear-to-ear grin that says she can't wait to put snakes in your bed. I like her right away.

I ask what's a good day for clouds, and she says it's when the clouds are white and moving around a lot. If I like, she'll show me the cloud game after breakfast.

We take the food outside and I put away the biggest breakfast—maybe the only breakfast—I've eaten in six months: three eggs, bacon, homemade hash browns and half a loaf of toast. Few things have ever tasted better.

A stretch of grass slopes down from where we're sitting to a big field of corn that gives way to blue hills in the distance. As we finish eating, a breeze comes up, and when the dishes are done, Luka takes me back outside for the cloud game.

We sit on the hill in her special spot, which is steep enough to lean against.

"Okay," she says. "This is the cloud game. As soon as you see a picture in the clouds you have to not-see it as fast as you can. You can do that one of two ways: look for another picture instead—but then you have to not-see that one too. Or change your looking so you see the whole sky all at once. When you're doing it that way, the little picture joins up with the big one and you don't get stuck as easy. Here's how to score: It's one point for every time you let go of a picture. But it's minus a point for every time you hold a picture for more than five seconds. Okay, *go*."

I look up and the first thing I see is the profile of a native American Indian chief, complete with feathered headdress, strong chin and straight nose. It's just about perfect, and I find it tricky to not-see it. I don't really want to not-see it, it's that good. But the wind blows the clouds around and soon the headdress rips off. Then the nose goes all bulgy and the chin flies away. I'm losing him, and to tell you the truth, I'm finding the whole thing pretty irritating.

I'm about to make a polite getaway when Luka says "You got stuck on the first picture, didn't you? I can tell because you're antsy. Don't give up—it's fun when you get the hang of it. Grandpa Jay says it's the best recipe for devil spinning when you're starting out."

It now strikes me that a twelve-year-old is talking to me as if everyone in the world knows about devil spinning. I ask what she means, and she says the cloud game gets you tossing the part that expects things to look a certain way.

"Every time you let go of a little picture, you get to go back to the big one," she says. "Things are moving all the time up there, so you can't get stuck. Try again; I'm already up to sixty-three."

I look up again, and this time I see a giraffe. I tell myself to let it go and sure enough, it disappears. For a moment I see nothing but shapes and motion on a big huge screen. I go back to the giraffe, then back to the big screen. If I don't linger long on any one shape, I can stay in the big one as long as I like. It feels pretty good. But when I stay too long in a little picture, I get annoyed when it gets wrecked. For a kid's game, it was pretty good. Gave me a nice stretchy feeling.

Luka won, of course. She was way ahead of me.

I could go on and on about my ten days in Wakeville. Seems like everywhere I go in this town there's someone giving me their recipe for devil spinning. They all have their favourite routines, and every one of them is something you do on purpose. None of them are things you can just think about.

Now you know I get around, Gabe. And just because I sing for my supper, it's not like I don't know a thing or two. I read. I know a few of the Buddha-basics—I majored in going with the flow. Mine might have a higher alcohol content than most, but so what? Flow is flow, the way I see it.

But these guys, they're taking it to the streets. They're *dramatizing* it. Where else do you see that, except in some poor knob who's dialled right out?

These folks are the boys and girls next door, Gabe. And they're doing it *on purpose.* And nobody in the whole damn town is raising so much as an eyebrow—*because they're all in on it.*

* * *

Before you know it, it's Saturday, and I'm committed to playing the dance. Posters all over town are inviting everyone to the August High and Dry Days celebration, and it looks like the whole town's coming.

I've been playing the bar in the evenings and spending most nights at Wyn's, or out on the farm with Noah. Everyone's keeping their doors open and I'm helping out where I can. By the end of the week, I've picked half a field of corn for Noah, sold cookies for Dougan and dug two wells with Wyn. A well-rounded week.

I'm feeling pretty good too, in spite of the fact that I'm still throwing back a lot of beer. I'm eating well, and after a few days, I'm sleeping well too. So who am I to argue? Life is good.

Until the night of the dance. It's funny how a few simple words can turn your life around. There are times when ignorance is bliss, Gabe. And I doubt that anyone has ever had as much right to that statement as me. I'll finish the story now and let you decide for yourself.

The dance gets off to a great start, and the whole town shows up for it. Everyone from three to a hundred-and-three is there, and there's enough food to feed two armies. They've been baking and cooking for days, and the tables in the hall are piled high with roast chickens and beef and ham, and potato salads and pies and cakes. There's kegs of beer for the grown-ups, soft drinks for the kids and tubs of fresh watermelon on every table.

It's a beautiful summer night and the hall doors are wide open so people can spill out onto the grass. Most of us are eating outside.

I'm hanging out with the boys in the band. We've been practicing through the week and everyone's pretty relaxed about the evening. These are local boys, so it's not like they have anything to prove. The people have come to dance, and they're going to give them everything they've got.

I'm just happy to be along for the ride. I'm having such a good time with my guitar, I'll go anywhere and play anything as long as I get to play. Everything I'm doing is fun, from blues to bluegrass to rock. I'm still on the hook of my runaway tune, but I'm not feeling urgent about it. I have the feeling it's willing to wait for me.

At about 8:30, they start moving tables and clearing the floor for dancing. We climb onstage to finish setting up, and we're just about to start when Billy the drummer does a little roll.

The lead singer, Clive, leans into the mike and asks if Noah Jay would please step up to kick off the dance.

Everyone claps as Noah surfaces, pint in hand, from the middle of the floor. Luka is pulling him from the front and another tow-headed youngster is pushing him from behind. He pretends to grumble as he climbs onstage.

"Short and sweet," he warns. "You folks have nabbed me for the speech three years running now, and I've used up all my speech words. So this is going to be quick."

He thanks everyone who's contributed to the great spread, and everyone who's helped with the decorating, and he thanks the band in advance for the music. He even gives me a welcome on behalf of the town.

Finally, he thanks us all for taking part in the August High and Dry Days. As he lifts his mug for a toast, he says "Dry is high, folks—and we can prove it! Here's to our tenth annual!" Everyone claps, and Billy gives another drumroll as Noah steps offstage.

The boys start playing and the dance gets underway, but I'm a little distracted by Noah's speech. Something doesn't sit quite right. I've been seeing the posters all week and assuming the High and Dry Days have to do with summertime and the harvest and all that. But now I'm not so sure. The speech made it sound like something else.

I put it out of my mind and focus on the music, but I'm a little off. Not bad, just not a hundred percent there.

When the first break comes, I head outside for some air. A part of me is burning to ask a question, but another part is thinking it might not be such a good idea. I run into Wyn having a beer, and as usual, my mouth decides for me.

"Wyn," I say, "What's this High and Dry business about anyway? What's the town celebrating?"

"Why Haley," he says, "It's our tenth dry August, like the sign says. The town stops drinking for the month of August every year."

"What? No, wait a minute," I say. "What about the beer?" I'd arrived in early August and I'd been drinking beer for ten straight days. We all had.

"Oh hell," says Wyn. "That's Nonny's No-Nod, Haley. Non-alcoholic. It tastes like beer, but there's no kick to it. You could drink a barrel of that and not feel a thing. It's just for those who like the taste of a beer."

"But why? Why would the whole town stop drinking for a month?"

"Well, it started with a dare. No, that's not quite true—it actually started with a dead dog. Ten years ago, Dougan ran over Noah's dog, Roper, after he'd had a few too many. Sad day. Noah loved that dog. The whole town loved Roper. He had the quiet in him, even as a pup. He could gentle any animal. He used to come to the bar with Noah and do the rounds. Put his chin on your knee, look in your eyes, pass on the quiet. A born devil spinner. When he died, Noah was sad for a long time.

"Then one day when he was walking down Main Street, something made him come to a stop. He swears it was Roper. He could see him standing off to the side, wagging his tail. When he walked over to him, Roper was gone but the wagging was still there. Like a vibration in the air. Noah says he could feel it all around him. He likened it to a time-spread, only with the wagging added. When he came out, he had the quiet back. And he's never lost it since. It's like Roper's still with him.

"But for Dougan it was different. Poor old Dougan couldn't forgive himself. Plus he kept thinking about what if it was a kid he ran over and all that. He couldn't get past it. He fell into drinking way too much, all the time. It was painful. Upset the whole town.

"Dougan had a fortuitous weak spot though—he couldn't resist a dare. So a few of us got together and dared him to stop for a month. We bet him five hundred bucks he couldn't do it. He said he could do it, no problem, but he didn't want to. We kept bugging him, saying maybe he wanted to all right, but maybe he couldn't.

"Then one day he up and did it. Stopped for a whole month.

But he was still pretty snarly by the end of it. And he didn't like being the only one on the wagon. So he dared the rest of us to stop for a month too. We hemmed and hawed, said we didn't need to, told him we didn't have the same problem. He said then it shouldn't be hard. Then he said if we'd stop for a month, he'd go for another month himself. He challenged the whole bar. Well, we wanted him to keep going, so we did.

"It wasn't that hard, either—especially with all of us doing it. Then Dougan dared us to do a second month if he did a third, and it went on like that for a while.

"It became a thing to spread the dare. Pretty soon the whole town was doing their month. Not that anyone said you had to. You were free to have a real drink anytime, but some of us wanted to see how long we could go.

"No one was in a big hurry to get back to real drinking either. Some did, some didn't. Some went back and forth. We were all still hanging out at the bar and some of us were happy with the No-Nod.

"But Dougan wasn't doing so well. Without the booze, he had nothing to ease his mind. He still wasn't drinking, which was good, but he stopped coming to the bar and he stopped hanging out with his friends. He just worked and holed up at home.

"By this time, Noah had the quiet back, and he wanted Dougan to be happy again. It was good how he went about it. He asked Dougan over for supper one night, and when they finished eating, he said it was time for him to call in Roper. Said he needed to find out for himself if the dog was holding a grudge. Dougan was having none of it at first. He had a lot of nervous ideas about how Roper felt about him. Then Noah double-dog-dared him—*ha!*—and he couldn't refuse.

"Dougan says when he called in Roper it was like he'd been waiting outside the door the whole time. He came right in and rested his furry old chin on Dougan's knee. (Well, Dougan says that's how it felt.) And he passed on the quiet to him, no hesitation, just like before.

"So Dougan got to make his peace. And that's when he got interested in devil spinning. He's always said the Roper method is best, but you have to be a dog. So he found his own way.

"We all got interested around that time. And one thing we all found out was that you can't do it drunk. Too much alcohol shoots your focus. And kills the quiet.

"After Dougan made his peace, we decided it would be nice to have a month every year where we all stopped drinking together. We picked August because that was Dougan's first dry month. Plus it's a great month for devil spinning.

"So that's how the August High and Dry Days came about. There won't be any real booze in town now till September."

* * *

I tell you Gabe, if anything ever pulled the rug out from under me, it was Wyn's words that night. You could have dropped me with a kiss. You could have decked me with a feather. I couldn't get it. I am a drinker, Gabe. I have not gone a day without alcohol in two decades.

I go into a kind of shock. Part of me is saying, "Hey, not bad, Haley—you just made it through ten days of not drinking without even knowing it," and another part is saying, "Haley, you're in big trouble—you've just gone ten days without a drink and that's something you can't do."

Billy comes by and holds up a hand to show me we're on in five. I drift toward the hall, and before I can think another thought, I'm back onstage.

I tell myself to focus on the music and sort out the rest of it later. And I manage all right through the first song. But then something happens to the sound. Or I think something happens. No one else looks bothered, but it sounds distorted to me. It's hardly noticeable at first, but after a while it gets right out of hand. Sludgy and thick one minute, brassy and harsh the next. Then way too fast, then way too slow.

I make the mistake of looking out at the dance floor. When the music is sludgy, people are swaying in huge undulating waves, like giant amoebas. When it's brassy, they're jerking and stuttering like they're under a strobe. But they're not.

It gets more and more difficult to play. It also gets harder to stay upright. I decide what I need is a drink. Without thinking, I reach for the pint on the speaker beside me. I take a long sip before I remember: *This is not real beer.* Then it hits me: *There is not a single real beer in this whole crazy town.*

I feel physically ill; I mean seriously nauseous. I decide I must be going through some kind of delayed withdrawal. Ten whole days without beer, and now nausea and hallucinations. *Jesus*, I think, *this must be the DTs.* My worst nightmare. What else could it be?

From that moment on, I'm a man with a mission. I have one goal in life and that is to get to a place where the beer is real.

I pretend to break a string and edge my way backstage. Then I slip down the side steps and head for the door. Most of the adults are dancing, and nobody sees me leave except Luka, who's on her way in as I go out.

She's going at a run, looking behind her, and she dives headfirst into my stomach. Knocks the wind right out of me.

She dusts me off and makes a fuss. Then she asks how come I'm not onstage. I tell her I'm going out for a little air. I say it's a good night for clouds and I'm going to try the cloud game by moonlight. She waves and says, "Don't get stuck on the first picture, Haley!"

* * *

And those are the last words I hear in Wakeville: "Don't get stuck on the first picture, Haley." Within ten minutes, I have my gear together and I'm walking past the Welcome to Wakeville sign. Within half an hour, I'm on the main highway with my thumb out, heading north. And within two hours, I'm in a roadside tavern I hope I never see again, with a real beer in each hand, waiting to get drunk.

And I *do* get drunk. Stinking, unsociably drunk. I sit in a corner drinking steadily till closing time. Anyone talks to me, I snarl. At midnight, I buy a six-pack for the road and get back on the highway.

No rides, so I drink half the pack while I'm walking. I pass out around 2:00 a.m. in a field by the side of the road, and when I wake up, I remember what hangovers are all about. The funny thing is, I can't for the life of me remember why I was in such a hurry to remember.

I think back to the night before, and it strikes me that I wasn't in such bad shape as I thought. In fact, when I think about it, the nausea and hallucinations hardly lasted past the point where I left the hall. I don't remember having them on the road out of town.

But I was so determined to get the hell out of Dodge, I didn't stop to notice. Maybe all I needed was some air after all. Maybe I'll never know. What I do know is that I have one hell of a hangover and only three beers to see me straight. I don't want to wake up in a field again tomorrow, so I stick out my thumb and head for Halifax.

I don't know why north, or why Halifax. I could've headed

south to Kittery Point like I planned. Maybe I just needed to be on familiar ground, and Halifax was the closest. But I don't even look up friends when I get there. I stay drunk for a week, playing a downtown liquor store and crashing at one of those smelly skid row shelters.

Then I get homesick for Vancouver. Nothing's making sense, especially staying drunk. Especially when I think about going ten days without a drink and not even knowing it. I tell you Gabe, there's a way worse hell than simple self-destruction. You can be stylish with self-destruction, flashy even, once you've accepted it, because you're not of two minds about what you're doing. You've made your peace and you don't believe it can be any other way.

The real hell is finding out it *can* be some other way, and not only that, it can be some other way quite painlessly—and then watching yourself go out and self-destruct anyway. Knowing you don't have to and still doing it—that's what I call hell, Gabe.

All I can think of to do now is retrace my steps. Get back to Vancouver and start fresh. Only now that I'm here, all I can think of to do is get back to Wakeville. That's where the trouble started. If I'm going to retrace my steps, maybe I have to do it all the way.

The problem is, I don't even know if I can find the place again. Google hasn't heard of it and it's such a small town, it isn't listed on any maps. I thought it got lost in a fold, but who knows? Maybe it doesn't exist. Maybe the whole ten days was a dream. Still, I figure I have to go looking for it sooner or later. I won't be getting much peace till I do.

Right now though, I've got to go play some tunes. Which brings up the other worst part: the music. For a while I really had it, but I've lost it again. The guitar feels dead. And that's how the songs come out. If I could get the music back, it wouldn't be so bad.

The thing is, if I hadn't got off in Wakeville that day, I'd be fine.

I'd be the same as before. Not exactly "adjusted," maybe—whatever that is—but more or less in one piece. I wouldn't have to know what I was missing.

***

It's after 8:00 o'clock now and Haley has to run if he wants to keep his spot at the liquor store. He's hardly touched his food but he doesn't even ask them to bag it. He just says goodbye and lopes across the street. I've never seen anyone looking so blue.

***

That's the last I saw of him until today. I kept looking for him through the winter, expecting him to show up at Crawley's and tell me how he nearly got to Wakeville. I never expected to run into him downtown.

But there he is at 3:00 o'clock this afternoon, in front of the old Virgin Records store. We're walking in the same direction at first, so l don't see him till I turn. He's marching past the windows at a real clip, eyes forward, and I could swear he's looking straight at me, but he doesn't see me. I'm about to call out when he suddenly comes to a halt, does a quick little turn and looks hard at the window.

I duck into the building so I can watch from the inside. He stands for about a minute in front of the glass, then turns and heads back down the sidewalk the other way.

I'm losing sight of him, so I go up to the second floor where I can see the whole block.

By now he's at the corner, doing another turn. He's wearing Dougan's crazy black outfit and doing his whole routine; I recognize the moves. His guitar case is open on the sidewalk about midway down the block, and there's a stool and a brown paper bag beside it. I'm guessing there's a mickey of vodka in the bag; that's what he usually has at the liquor store.

I decide to go down to the street and do a pass, see if he notices me. He sees me from half a block away, I can tell by the sideways grin.

Once we're in range, he reaches his hands out. Without thinking, I reach back, like we're partners in a square dance. I'm dying to start laughing or make a run for it. I just know he's going to make me do something funny.

And I'm right. He locks eyes with me, then leans back so I have to lean back too. Once we're balancing toe to toe, he starts swinging me around, slowly at first, then faster and faster. After a minute, when I'm good and dizzy, he slows me down and brings me in for a landing. Then he turns me so I'm facing the window and the world comes spinning in, all upside down and inside out. I know I'm in there somewhere, but I'm hard-pressed to place myself.

Now in a loud stage whisper, he says, "Okay Gabe, here's where we step to the side and make time wide."

He takes my hands and we do the little sidestep, like we're climbing out of the tub. We stand quietly for a moment, then he lets me go and I follow his moves. We raise our arms slowly and make the V, then we stand on tiptoe with our legs apart and make the X. Once we're stretched as high and wide as we can get, we just hang, nice and still, for about three minutes. I can feel us going into the time-spread.

There's a lot I could say about that part, but it might take a whole book. And this is Haley's story, not mine. What I will say is that when I'm in it, I see things differently. Haley especially. I can't put my finger on it at first. There's the crazy costume and the Dougan moves, but that's not it. It's more like something's missing. Then I realize. He's lost the background roar. And passed along the quiet.

We step out and he gives me a little kiss on the cheek. I say, "Good to see you, Haley."

He says, "Good to be seen, Gabe."

We go over to where he's left his stuff and he picks up the guitar. When he moves the stool, I notice there's a pint of milk and a half-eaten sandwich in the bag. No vodka. I plant myself on the sidewalk with my back to the wall. I want to hear what he's got.

Turns out I'm there for the rest of the afternoon, till I have to run or be late for work. I really don't want to go. Partly because of the music, and partly because I don't know if I'll be seeing Haley again. But he waves when I get up to go and tells me he'll be coming by Crawley's soon. Then he calls out "Wakey-wakey, Gabe!" as I'm rounding the corner.

I never did get a chance to ask him where he got to last, but I figure it doesn't matter. It doesn't matter what anyone else thinks, either, or if anyone ever believes his story. The important thing, the way I see it, is that Haley made it back to Wakeville. One way or another.

JIMMY THE PACER

JIMMY THE PACER

Haley shows up at Crawley's the day after our sidewalk encounter, with Dutch and Sam right on his heels. The place erupts in hoots and hollers; it's the first time in over a year that the three of them have been in the same place at the same time.

They spread themselves out around the loop of the shoe—the sweet spot of the stand-up bar—and just as the travel tales have begun to fly, Jimmy the Pacer walks in. The boys shuffle over to make room for him by the self-serve counter, which is where he likes to stand while he gets his bearings.

Jimmy is a tall, sandy-haired man in his mid-forties who's been a regular at Crawley's for about six years. You might say he's a bit of a traveler himself. He chats with you briefly while he buys his first pint, and he's always politely flirtatious. If you're one of the female bartenders, he might tell you you're looking cuter than a bug's left ear and ask you what's new. Then he'll report that he's been up in the Interior panning for gold, or out at the university working on some new invention. Then he'll ask you what's new again.

He doesn't generally leave you any room to talk back in—just rattles along while you're pouring his beer. Then he leans in a long diagonal sprawl across the bar and looks around. He wears a cowboy hat pulled down over his eyes so he has to tilt his head back to see out, and when he's down to about half a pint, he starts pacing.

I'm curious to see if he'll join in the travel talk with the boys. Sam has been telling a story about a trip he made to Peru in mid-April. He and Dutch have been shipping out on freighters for the past year, mainly to South America. They're both working on their master's tickets and they need the deep-sea time.

Sam's tale is about an encounter he had on a beach in the port of Callao. It was his birthday and he'd gone ashore with a few of the dockworkers, intending to be back by dark. But once his comrades learned that it was his birthday, there was no getting away till the wee hours.

When he finally got back to the docks, he was completely turned around. He figured it was hopeless—and probably dangerous—to start looking for his ship in the dark. The security in Callao is intense and the docks go on for miles, so he didn't want to get caught roaming around.

As he pondered what to do next, he caught sight of a large black lump on a nearby stretch of beach, which he recognized as an overturned lifeboat he'd noticed the day before. Since the nights were still warm and dry, he decided to take cover under it for the night and make his way back to his ship in the morning.

"It never occurred to me that it might be occupied," he said.

As he was crawling under the boat, he heard a woman shriek. "I mean *shriek*-shriek," he said. This scared him half to death, so he let out a yell. The woman then shrieked even louder and Sam yelled louder. Then they both recoiled and whacked the backs of their heads on the gunnels of the boat. "Practically cracked both our skulls," Sam said.

They yelped in unison this time and collapsed in heaps on either side of the boat. Sam said the woman must have crossed herself a hundred times and he must have yelled *"Pardonnez-moi!"* a hundred times. Unfortunately, she did not speak French.

"Not *loud* French, anyway," said Sam. "...which is just as well because that was all I had."

Once Sam found a way to explain that he was lost and meant her no harm, the woman recovered and kindly made room for him. As it turned out, she was living under the boat.

"You could tell too," said Sam. "The place had a real woman's touch. Little driftwood crosses hanging from the gunnels, family photos and pictures of Jesus taped to the hull. Even a couple of candles and a bit of worn rug."

They had a polite conversation in English and Spanish, which neither of them could understand. "... And no hanky-panky either," said Sam. "Just for the record."

She even made him coffee in the morning. "A really nice lady," he said.

"I know a nice lady," says Jimmy, and we all turn his way. He's nodding slowly, as if about to launch, but it's hard to know with Jimmy. The boys nod and wait, and Jimmy nods and waits. Then just as Haley's about to take a turn, Jimmy says, "She lives in a van on one of those little side streets off Terminal Avenue. Right-side up, though. The van I mean. The lady's right-side up too, most of the time.

"You don't want to climb into her van, though," he warns. "Not if she didn't invite you first. Nobody does that unless they're really dumb... And *oboy*, you should hear her if they do. She's got a scream on her could make your blood run cold in a hot spring. So don't say I didn't warn you."

The boys nod soberly, and Jimmy tips his hat. Then he starts to pace. Around the curve of the bar toward the washrooms, then around the other way past the windows, then back. After a short while, he finds the right routine and settles into it. It's usually back and forth across the windows for the main stretch—about thirty feet—then a couple of passes along the wall—about twenty feet—then back to the windows. He's not social at all once he's got his rhythm up. Just keeps to his path with the same long stride and his hat down over his eyes.

Everyone stops noticing Jimmy once he's into his routine, unless they're new to the bar. Except for this day. On this day, for some reason, he uses the wall stretch for his main route, pacing from the washrooms to the door and back. It being a warm day, the door is propped wide open.

After about fifteen minutes, Jimmy has settled into his routine and become pretty much invisible. By now the bar has begun to fill and I'm getting into a rhythm of my own.

Then suddenly something feels wrong. The bass goes out of the bar noise and there's a funny hush in the air. It's as if someone's been messing with the sound system, but I know that's not the case. A few of the regulars start looking vaguely around, but there's nothing much to see. Then Haley turns his head to the street, and I look outside.

Well. There's Jimmy on the sidewalk, pint in hand, looking like he's landed on Mars when he expected to be somewhere near the washrooms at Crawley's. He's lost his place and paced himself right out the door.

People are trying not to stare, but you can tell that half the bar is on hold. I'm pretending not to notice because I don't want to go out and tell Jimmy he's not supposed to drink on the sidewalk. I know he's out there by mistake—Jimmy's not a defiant type—and I don't want to add embarrassment to his bewilderment. But I'm also hoping no cops come by.

I finally send a silent SOS to the boys, and a minute later Haley wanders outside. "Hey Jimmy," he says. "They'll pop you for sure if they catch you out here with that beer. You better do your drinking inside."

Jimmy ponders this for a moment, then gives Haley a nod. He tilts his head back to drain the last of his pint and sets his glass down carefully in the flowerbed. Then he walks back in and steps up to the bar like he's coming in for the first time today.

"Gabe," he says. "What's new? Did anyone ever tell you you're cuter than a bug's left ear?" I say hiya Jimmy and he tells me he's working on a project out at UBC that's going to let you harness the airflow from an everyday household fan so you can store it in a car battery and run your car by remote anywhere in a radius of fifteen miles from your house. And this will handle the energy crisis and maybe put Canada on the map for a change.

"Hey, eat your heart out, Elon," I say and wish him luck. He says thanks, then picks up his pint and begins his walk. This time he starts with the window side.

I give Haley a juice on the house and for the next few minutes we keep an eye on Jimmy to be sure he stays on course. You can tell the whole bar is doing the same.

He gets his rhythm up in no time and goes back to being invisible in the usual way.

Dutch and Sam make plans to hook up with Haley later in the evening and head out. Then Haley moves over to Jimmy's spot, where it's easier to chat.

"There's something kind of soothing about watching Jimmy pace," he says. "Puts a nice rhythm in all the hubbalub."

"Yeah, Jimmy's all right," I say. *(Hubbalub?)* "Why do you think he paces?"

"Oh, I guess he's spinning out his devils like the rest of us," says Haley. "Everyone's a devil spinner, Gabe—one way or another. Formulas vary, of course. Some set you free; some don't."

"What kind is Jimmy's, do you think?"

"Couldn't say for anyone but me," says Haley. "Maybe it's a

bit of both. Or maybe it depends on the day. Sometimes we spin to make the needle skip, sometimes we spin for the comfort of the groove."

"But all in all, do you think he's doing okay?"

"Yeah, I do. Everyone thinks Jimmy's needle is stuck, but who knows what an afternoon of pacing is doing for him? He might be spinning out devils that would keep you or me in a straitjacket for life.

"Speaking of grooves," he adds, "I'm on at the liquor store in five. And you know what? I'm looking forward to it."

By now it's nearly 4:00, and the place is starting to hum. Haley says goodbye and it makes me happy to see the spring in his step. You can tell he still has the music.

As I'm gearing up for rush hour, I start wondering what I do to make the needle skip. And what I do that's just for the comfort of the groove.

Jimmy comes up for a fresh pint, and I give him a big smile.

"You put a nice rhythm in all the hubballub, Jimmy."

"Thanks Gabe," he says. "So do you," Then he gets on with his walk, and I realize it's my job, on both counts.

FRANK EMAIL ENDS BADLY

(Napkinalia # 1)[1]

[1]*Napkinalia: Words scrawled on bar napkins*

FRANK EMAIL ENDS BADLY

(Napkinalia # 1)

~~Dear Frank,~~
~~Hi Frank,~~
~~Hello Frank,~~
~~Frank, hello.~~
~~Hiya Frank,~~
~~Hey Frankie,~~

(sheesh)

Frank,
~~Hope you're enjoying this lovely summer weath...~~
~~How's it going?~~
~~What's up?~~

(jeez)

~~I enjoyed meeting you for coffee and~~... *(what? and nothing)*
I enjoyed our coffee.
~~Your point about the lack of transparency, often ignored or only obliquely referenced in current critiques of the~~

~~post-postmodern conclusion that all deconstructions are necessarily, by dint of having been made, constructions themselves, raises the question~~…

(omfg)

~~I do understand that a formal deconstruction may itself be considered a construction of sorts, and therefore subject (endlessly) to further deconstruction, but loops such as these tend to arise from confusing class with member. Guidelines for logical typing suggest~~ ...

(aarrgh, shoot me)

~~I'll be in your neighbourhood Thursday~~... *(*no*)*
~~If you're in the downtown area again~~ ... *(nah)*
~~You might be interested in an event I'm hosting~~… (nope*)*

Frank, I enjoyed our coffee. You have a great ass. *(Ha!)*

(Fuck this.)
(Fuck you Frank.)

CROWS

CROWS

So this is where you live. I must have passed this way a dozen times, browsing for wood on your beach. I wonder if I'll know the place in daylight.

You run ahead to turn on lights, warning me to be careful; the second step is not nailed in. I climb up worn wooden planks, inhaling the smell of fresh-cut cedar from the kindling on your stoop.

A row of nails lines the wall of the mudroom—thick strong nails for hanging heavy coats. I would have struggled with screw-in pegs and cursed them for getting loose in a week.

I take off my boots and pad through the open door.

We're scrubbed up and foolish, ignoring the background maybe. Pretending this is everyday stuff—not two nearly-strangers, past middle age, wondering if it's worth all this. I picture myself getting away in an hour or two. Breaking into a crazy gallop like a ten-year-old. Rearing and snorting and yipping it all away.

A pair of long grey socks dangles from a nail above your stove. Hand-wrung, drying in a twist with the toes turned out. The sight of them tugs at me alarmingly.

You men and your nails. I turn away.

It's different having a date. Not at all like the idle banter at Crawley's. That's where we met. I tend bar there and you sometimes come by for a pint when you're in Vancouver.

But this is different. I've been house-sitting down the way at my cousin's cabin, and I had no idea you lived around here. We met by chance on the beach and made a date.

We've been to a movie at Shirley Hall, assessed it superficially, hardly looked at one another all evening.

I have a chance now. Your back is to me, bent over a tray of tea things. You're making us a snack, and it's warm milk, not tea; I see you lift the skin off with a finger. My eyes rest for a moment on the curve of your back, where the fabric is smooth. It's a nice back, I think; I couldn't say why.

You carry the tray to a long wooden table in the middle of the room. I like the open layout, the main room one big kitchen. A space for visiting and doing things. The living room is at the far end, in front of the fireplace. Two overstuffed chairs and a sofa, more intimate. I'm glad we're in the kitchen part.

I glance at your face as you set down plates and mugs. You are safely absorbed in your task. Your work-rough hands look strange among the dishes, taking such care. Dwarfing the little slabs of bread and cheese. I look away; I don't want to see you make a fuss. I'd rather see you slap the tray down, slop the milk a little and spill some.

"Ah! Nearly forgot the pièce de résistance!"

You twirl back to the counter, swoop up a jar of honey and plant it with mock precision in the middle of the table.

"Do you like your milk with honey?"

I confess I've never tried, and you feign disdain.

Now I kind of like that you're making this proper, flirting safely with tasty offerings. I smile in your direction.

You escort me to the table and tuck in my chair. Then you sit down across from me and size things up. Nothing appears to be missing. Still, you hesitate.

"Music? I have music...?"

"I like hearing the ocean, if that's okay."

"Good. Me too."

You sit back down and flash me a goofy grin. There's nothing more to do. I spoon out honey and pass you the jar.

"It's nice here," I say.

"I think so. Nicer than anywhere else I've been."

"Any wild animals?"

"Well there's sand fleas in high tides. Water rats, raccoons. But they're polite if you leave them be. The biggest worry is logs. Strays from the booms get thrown up the beach from time to time. Mostly in high tides, late in the year. My neighbour had one shoot straight through his living room a couple of Christmases ago. We put barricades up in the winter now."

I ask how long you've lived here, where you were last, what you've done for work. Mostly you've worked on boats—coastal freighters, towboats, the odd deep-sea trip. You have a mate's ticket, but it doesn't get much use. You like being on deck. The work is healthy, the money is decent, and your time off is your own.

I'm struck by how at peace you are with work. No talk of good guys and bad guys, no complaints about working conditions. A nice change from the usual bar talk.

I'm also struck by how you speak. My questions are routine, designed to get you talking. Your responses are brief, almost curt, as if you're waiting for me to change the channel. You don't seem to mind the pauses; I find them awkward. We're in one now.

I'm quite a nervous person, though you wouldn't know it to see me at the bar. I'm chatty there. Serving is an easy groove and I play a bit part. Most of the time I'm just a fly on the wall.

Everyone gets nervous sometimes, I know that. But it feels more serious with me. I don't just get the odd butterfly. I get crows—cartoons of crows, actually. Hundreds of them, flapping and squawking and swooping around in my head. I've got them now. There's a little cartoon lady too. She looks like Mister Magoo, only with curlers and a housecoat. The crows are in the lady's garden and she's trying to shoo them out with a broom. They flap just out of reach, then settle back down as soon as she turns away.

Makes it hard to think.

I assumed you'd do most of the talking. How retro. But isn't that what men do? Maybe not so much these days. Except in bars. It's what men used to do when I was growing up. And the women encouraged it. The women would get them talking and settle back to observe. Then chuckle fondly over coffee about their self-centred men.

Am I doing what my mother did? *Yikes.* I can still see her in our old front room, being gracious. She and her cousins went to finishing school. When they turned eighteen, they were sent abroad to learn the social graces.

Which reminds me—I watched a woman in the bar commit social suicide last week. She came in with her partner and a bunch of his workmates. The only woman at the table. The men were all in the trades and they were telling funny stories about work. At some point the woman said something outrageously funny herself. Funnier than anything anyone else had said. I was bussing the next table and I heard every word.

Amazingly, not one of the men acknowledged it; not even her partner. No one laughed. No one even looked her way. They just went on with their work stories.

She went red at first and got very quiet. Then she got mad. I could see the whole catastrophe brewing. I wanted to yell *"No!"* and drag her away from the table. But of course I couldn't. She waited for a pause, then she said, "You know, what I just said was funny. Really funny, actually. And not one of you acknowledged it. Not one of you even looked my way."

I wanted to weep. Her partner looked down. The table was silent for half a beat, then they went back to their conversation, partner included, as if she hadn't spoken. She sat for a few more seconds, then picked up her bag and walked out.

Crap, why am I thinking about this now? That poor woman—so right and yet so wrong. You can bet she never went to finishing school. My God, what a name for a school. They actually called it charm school in some places. I can see them all on graduation day—rows and rows of bright-shiny-apple girls with bright-shiny-apple smiles, waving their little certificates. Officially finished. Certifiably polished off.

I want to laugh now. A big snorty messy laugh. This is ridiculous. What am I doing here? People are such a sorry mess. Even the brightest. Better to be a fly on the wall.

I have no idea what you said last. I think you asked me a question. Something to do with history. I need to grace up, say something smart. I am dangerously close to laughing.

How about that Trump.

Gosh, this global warming business is a nuisance.

Done much therapy?

Jesus-Mary-and-Joseph. *Do not laugh.*

"Sorry," I say. "I got distracted for a moment."

You shrug.

"I'm blaming age; I spaced right out."

"You're back now though, aren't you?"

"Yes, but I lost our place. You were asking me something... ?"

"I was asking if it was crucial for you to know my whole history all at once. I mean it's nice of you to take an interest, but I have some resistance to interviews—unless I'm applying for work. Everything gets so abridged."

"What do you mean?" *I know exactly what you mean.*

"I mean I prefer to discuss my history when something interesting brings it up. The facts by themselves are so bland. They need context. They need to be seasoned by the stories that go with them."

"Was I rushing you past your stories?" *Of course I was.*

"Not intentionally, I'm sure. Don't get me wrong—I don't want to tell you all my stories either. It's just that if a story should come up, it might need a little time. Good stories usually do. But the rapid-fire format isn't exactly conducive. You can't just pull a story off the shelf and slap it on the table like a can of beans. Can-of-bean stories are gap-fillers. Or one-up contests. They really crowd the table."

I think of my tradesmen piling up their stories, one on top of another. Not even waiting for the last one to land before the next one begins. Definitely a crowded table.

"Did you think I was asking for can-of-bean stories?"

"Maybe not, but it did feel like you were still at work. I was hoping to catch a glimpse of the woman behind the bar. Maybe ask her a question or two. Like 'when does she get off work?' Or 'does she like ice cream?' We have some."

You're smiling. I'd like to say something gracious, but the crows are back. I can't think. Can't find my Magoo-lady either. Maybe I've lost her. Maybe she's tired of the neighbourhood. I know I am.

"Hey," you say. "You took off again. Come back." You reach across the table and brush my cheek with the back of your fingers.

"I'm here."

"Good. Welcome back."

I stick out my tongue. Which, oddly, feels better. The crows fly off to the back of the garden.

"Your track was probably more interesting anyway."

"Only if you like chasing crows." *I couldn't begin.*

You give me a quizzical look, then soften. "Hey, I'm a bastard. I knock you off your perch and then I go and rattle your cage. Look out for me; I'm not to be trusted."

Something is happening. My shoulders drop and I realize I was holding them up. I begin to laugh, but stop myself. Laughing would take me away right now.

Something is happening that I don't want to miss. Something that feels easy, but couldn't be. It's like we're coming to a place where there are no crows.

No, that's not it. The crows are still there, but I'm feeling no need to chase them. Maybe they're like your water rats and coons—polite if you leave them be.

There's an easy quiet between us now, with nothing flapping to fill it up. I look at your face. It is a face without contortions, willing to hold my gaze. Willing to wait for me through the nervousness, the routine. The impulse to run.

My heart feels too big for its cage. Without thinking, I get up and walk over to your chair. I bend across your back and stretch my arms along the length of yours, burying my face in the hollow of your neck. You turn and touch your cheek to mine, then rock me gently from side to side.

***

Tomorrow it will all begin again. Crow flurries predicted. Tomorrow I'll be convinced that this hasn't happened; not to me, not like this. I will know that it couldn't happen again. I will listen for whispers to feed my doubt, and I'll feed my doubt to the crows.

Tomorrow I will do what I can to make nothing of this. I'll affect an indifference that will sting like a slap. You will wonder if I'm the same person you held through the night, and you will be chilled by my crisp goodbye.

Tomorrow, in spite of myself, I will call and invite you for dinner. Already I am hoping you will wait for me again.

LITTLE SISTER

LITTLE SISTER

Just a bug, she said when he saw the spider. *Can't hurtya.*

Just a joke, as he dropped his glass, splashed coke all over his jeans.

You can even swallow 'em, they're not dirty like flies.

The look he gave her, pure evil, as he slapped away the paper towels, the fluttering hands, the big-sister fuss.

He stood up slowly, eyes in slits. Walked right out of the house.

Nobody can take a joke around here! Didn't think he'd be scared of a stupid spider. Didn't think my sister would get a sissy for a boyfriend!

She crouches against the swats and slaps, propelled by sister-fury. Skids to the edge of the porch, jumps the five steps and lands in a sprawl on the grass.

You go after him and say you're sorry! Really *sorry!* Now! *And put this on—you're not decent!*

Her daddy's summer jacket flies after her, lands in a loop around her neck.

He's way ahead now, swaggering down the lane all nonchalant disgust. She staggers to her feet, puts the coat on like a cape, trudges through the summer dusk. He was supposed to stay for supper; her sister made it specially. And there was pie. She won't get any now.

She sulks behind, kicking a rock. Expecting him to stop and wait.

He keeps walking; he won't make it easy.

He's past the bend in the lane when she ditches the rock, puts her head down, runs full tilt. Runs right into him, waiting all dark and sly, all tall and quiet in the shadows.

Jeez! Arms flapping, heart slamming. *Fuck, man!* Feet stomping.

He looks at her like she's a bug.

What do you *want?*

She bends down, tries to heave a sulky-pissy sigh. Runs out of air.

I'm s'posed to say I'm sorry, and I didn't mean to scare you, and I didn't mean you to spill your stupid coke, and blahbitty-blah-blah.

He smirks, arms crossed, legs wide. Towering, all full of himself. She punches him. Can't help it. Once, twice, right in the gut, breath still raggedy, hard as she can. He doesn't budge, just shakes his head.

Pitiful.

She curses, gives it another shot, high, to the chin. Strikes air as he ducks.

Her daddy's summer jacket falls away and hits the ground.

Crap.

Her tidy sun-browned shape now outlined in the soft pink light. Arms and legs made darker by the white of the cotton singlet she wears like a dress in the heat.

She tugs at the front and looks down. Tugs at the back and frowns; the hem not even halfway to her knees.

He watches the rising-falling-rising of her rabbit-chest. Surprised by the rush. Surprised to be knocked off his cool.

For a moment nothing breathes. Then both reach down, bump heads and laugh.

He snatches the jacket, waves it over her head. Makes her jump, then bumps her sideways to the grass.

No fair!

Crybaby!

He hauls her up, clamps the jacket on her shoulders. Wags her from side to side.

You sure *you're sorry?*

Lifts out her hair, grabs it in a fist. Pulls back her head.

Really *sorry?*

His other hand stroking her throat, gently choking as she tries to nod.

I could strangle you right here and now, you know that?

Pinning her arms behind her as she tries to hit. Scorning her twists and turns.

Who's scared now, little sister?

Mimicking her yowls, her feeble *you-just-waits.* Knocking her softly around.

You give?

A barely perceptible nod as she goes limp.

He gives back an arm, pinches her nose, gives back the other arm. Pushes her away.

She stands and frowns. Waiting. Not running, not knowing why.

He smiles and watches; one beat, two. Then takes her by her daddy's lapels. Roughly, as if to shake her up. As if to show her what.

She braces and he smiles again, relaxes his grip. Rocks her back and forth. Then stands her still and holds her gaze.

She sways, about to tip. Reaches up to grab his arms. The jacket falls again and no one picks it up.

He holds her steady as she finds her feet, then tightens his grip. Pulls her close.

She looks up, startled. *Holy shit.*

Now knowing.

Her sister once explained about boys, but she only half listened. The subject made her squirmy.

Crap. What was it? Something about timing. *It's all in the timing*, her sister had said. She'd learned all about it when she worked in that bar with the creepy-crawly name.

He locks her wrists behind her back and leans in. His face looks huge. *Doesn't matter how small you are if you get the timing right.* She leans back slowly, shifts her weight to one leg and flexes the opposite knee. *But make it good. You won't get two chances.*

She slithers and pivots, slippery as an eel. Then bends the knee and drives it home.

Wait for the recoil, her sister had said. *The release comes right after. Then run for it. Don't let the yelling freak you out. Just keep running till you get somewhere safe.*

He falls back with a murderous yowl. *Recoil.* Then loses his grip. *Release.* She dives for the jacket and runs like the wind. She can still hear him yelling as she flies up the steps.

Home free.

The TV is on loud. Cops and robbers—good. The screen door slams behind her.

Well? Sister still fuming, arms all crossed, looking down her nose.

She grins, still panting. *Well what?*

Did you say you were sorry?

Yeah.

And?

He's sorry too.

For what?

For being such a sissy. What else?

PREVENTIVE MAINTENANCE

PREVENTIVE MAINTENANCE

Hey. Did you hear Matt's lost it again?

Whoa, already?

Yup. They frogmarched him out of the Depot yesterday. New strain of burnout.

Bummer.

No shit. Three strikes; he's toast. Poor guy couldn't build immunity.

Man, after all this time. He must've been with the Depot forever.

Eight years and counting.

Jeez—and I just passed probation a month ago.

Don't change your socks, kiddo.

What do you think comes first with Matt—the expectation or the meltdown?

What do you mean?

Well, does he lose it because he expects to lose it, or does he just lose it?

Who knows? Probably a bit of both. The better question is, would he keep on losing it if it weren't for the Weekly Warnings. Everyone's doing something on that list. I think he gets so freaked out about freaking out that he freaks out—again. It turns into a loop.

But the last warning expressly says DON'T FREAK OUT ABOUT FREAKING OUT. They know it can turn into a loop. Isn't that what the will pills are for? If he was freaking out about freaking out he should've gone to the dispensary. Besides, you don't catch a meltdown just from reading a list of warnings about possible symptoms.

I don't know. A guy could be walking around with all kinds of stuff—depression, anxiety, paranoia, all the different strains of burnout. As long as he doesn't know better, he figures he's just having the usual ups and downs. But let's say he hears about one in particular. It rings a bit of a bell. He starts monitoring himself more and more closely. It gets a little obsessive. Then some kind of last-straw thing happens—his wife leaves him, or his dog dies. Now he's ripe. Then *Bam!* Wave becomes particle. Overnight, the guy's got a full-blown case of whatever.

But not in the Depot, surely. Don't they screen for obsessive self-monitoring? If Matt was that susceptible, he'd never have got in the door. Third Warning: BE WISE, DESENSITIZE. I mean don't get me wrong, the warnings spook me too. But in a three-strike system, aren't you more likely to go into denial?

Smarter maybe; more likely I doubt. You tend to do the unsmart thing when you're freaking out. Besides, denial's on the list too. If you know you're in denial, you're supposed to take a reality pill.

Which would confirm you're having a meltdown, right? Bit of a Catch-22.

Exactly. So you're better off denying you're in denial. Which, you'll notice, is *not* on the list.

I did notice; I thought it was an omission. Isn't that a total contradiction?

Not really. Denying one denial is efficient—if it ends in a positive. No wasted bandwidth, no interruption to workflow. But one more denial could lead to looping—which is *definitely* on the list. It's all about knowing where to stop, my friend. That takes discipline. And *that* builds immunity.

Tell me. I fell into looping my first week on the job. I started thinking I was tired. (Second Warning: DO NOT ATTEND TO STRAY THOUGHTS). But I'm new, and I'm nervous, so I immediately think: No, I am not *tired. Which would've been fine, now that I think of it. (One denial, ending in a positive, right?) But no, now I think oh-oh, I'm in denial, which means I'm supposed to take a reality pill. If I'd denied I was in denial and stopped right there, I might've still been fine. But I hadn't got the hang of thought-stop yet.*

So what happened?

I started thinking, yow, *a reality pill could prove I really am tired—and that could get me fired. More stray thoughts, right? And the clock is ticking. Now I start thinking about how I can't stop thinking about how much I'm thinking—which, bottom line (Fourth Warning), means I'm cheating the Depot (YOU GET PAID FOR YOUR ATTENTION). Which will get me fired even faster than being tired. So I start denying I'm thinking about thinking, then denying I'm denying, and... Well, you get the picture. Talk about looping. I burned a whole day's bandwidth in under an hour. Had to make up an emergency and go home.*

Huh, smart. Speaking of burning bandwidth, R & D is using Matt in a case study. He's got this wild new strain of burnout. Apparently his brain was eating 185 bits of bandwidth per second—not just now and then, but routinely—for eight weeks before his meltdown.

No way. That's not even possible. Nobody burns that much.

Besides, if it was possible, and they knew about it, why would they let him do it? First warning: CONSERVE YOUR BANDWITH. More than 120 bits and you blow your brain's capacity to process.

So they thought. But he was hooked up to all the same equipment as us, and the meter was perfectly calibrated—allegedly. So they're saying the findings are legit. And you know what that means. There will be expectations, my friend. There will be expectations.

Crap. *I can't even break 115. That's my total max on a good day. What the heck happened to Matt?*

Well, first his capacity zoomed—like to superhuman—and then it tanked to 40 bits per second. Which they're saying is possibly temporary. They've got him in rehab.

Yikes, that should be fun. So are we expecting to see new warnings next week?

Not next week, but soon. Blake from HR had one too many at Crawley's last night and showed me a first draft. But they need more data. They need to find out if Matt's ahead of the curve or just an anomaly. If he turns out to be the first in a trend, they have to find out if his condition's exploitable. If it is, the symptoms will be written up as possible-positives. If he's anomalous or the condition's not exploitable, they'll be written up as probable-negatives. So no new warnings till they have their spin.

What are the symptoms? I mean aside from burning an insane amount of bandwidth?

Well, if you're like Matt, you start believing the things around you—desks, chairs, computers, what have you—are making unreasonable demands. Chairs demand to be sat on, floors to be walked on, doors to be opened and so on. The demands are quiet at first, more like subtle impulses, so you hardly notice. You figure they're harmless and you comply without thinking.

Big mistake—once the thing gets a toehold, it escalates. And each new compliance eats more bandwidth. When you're close to the breaking point, it feels like everything's competing with everything else for your attention. Very distracting.

The worst of it is, once you're burning over 150 bits, some kind of cybernetic override kicks in—an unforeseen glitch, apparently—that interferes with thought-stop. If you try to use it, the demands get even louder and nastier. Matt's solution was to keep adding tasks to his workload—which was already maxed—so he could tune out the noise. Of course, the Depot loved it—for all of eight weeks. The problem was, every day his bandwidth got stretched just a little bit more and a little bit more, till it finally snapped.

Brutal. Do they know what the cause is?

Well, aside from the glitch, which they're hoping to harness, they say just the everyday pressures of cyber-life. "They" being the new Mental Health Association. The CEO is Ira Krank, former energy consultant with TexxonGlobal. He's restructuring the MHA to conform with Texxon's business model. All mental conditions are being reclassified as either enhancements or interruptions to energy extraction.

Are you serious? That's ridiculous. They can't use a model for energy-extraction on mental health. It's apples and oranges.

Oh, they have their logic. Every disorder is being analyzed for actual or potential energy loss, measureable through bandwidth testing. Which means every subject is being classified as either a sound or an unsound conduit. We get paid for our attention, right? Fourth Warning, like you said. Well, "energy flows where attention goes." If your attention is focused on the right tasks and you're optimizing your bandwidth, you're classified CS—"Conduit-Sound." If your attention is scattered and you're wasting your bandwidth, you're classified CD—"Conduit-Defective."

But we're talking about burnout here. Does rehab include therapy, or any kind of counselling?

Sure, in the form of conduit upgrades—new thought-stop techniques, clean-machine workups, better-living-through-chemistry seminars, yadda-yadda. They call it Preventive Maintenance now. They say it's the fastest way to get workers back in the saddle. (Or eject them if they can't make the cut.) Bottom line, it's all about optimizing bandwidth.

But don't you find it kind of weird that bandwidth burnout didn't even exist a year ago? I mean outside the Depot?

Weird, definitely; surprising, not so much. Watch and learn—a hundred bucks says we're looking down the barrel—or should I say birth canal—of the latest corporate confection: "Mysterious pandemic of bandwidth burnout has employees leaving the workforce in droves." Then: "Social Services are so overwhelmed that Western nations are declaring a state of emergency." Then (are you ready?) "Government leaders reluctantly announce that privatization is the only key to saving the social net..."

Which by then will be shredded.

Let's just say "outsourced." Front-line Social Service jobs—and wages—will be slashed, leaving a very big slice of the pie for a very select group of corporate contractors. Who will manage to prove that all fallen-robin funds—including unemployment insurance—were needed in their massive restructuring. (Which will be labyrinthine in complexity, if anyone tries to follow the money.) It's Hurricane Katrina and all her successors showing up right on time. Nothing like the biggest disasters in history to distract us from the biggest disasters in history.

The plot is thickening, my friend. They said they were going to protect our jobs, but we all knew the jobs weren't there to protect. So this is what they're doing about it.

What? Declaring half the workforce defective?

Divide and conquer, amigo. With half the workforce gone, the Conduit Intacts will be the new elites—for as long as they can keep up. Another hundred bucks says they don't replace Matt—unless, of course, his condition turns out to be exploitable.

But everyone knows burnout is caused by overwork.

Do they? Read the new Diagnostics. They're saying burnout is not caused by overwork, or bandwidth monitoring, or warning lists. It's caused—so they say—by the subject's inability to manage his resources. Like what happened with Matt. His attention got so fractured that he fried; but not immediately. Not, in fact, for eight whole weeks.

All that added pressure actually made him more productive for a time—which is why they're so interested in him. Krank is an expert on fracking. He claims that all energy works on the same principles; they just haven't applied them properly to humans.

We all know attention is our primary resource, but the fracturing of it has been pretty primitive so far. Intentional fracking is crudely used by marketers in public spaces, the web being one. (Well, let's be accurate: the web being trillions.) And it works very well. When attention is fractured in the usual way—think giant flat-screens flickering from the walls of every mall—we get distracted and agitated. Which makes us perfect consumers—a little anxious, a little hungry for something we can't quite nail... and chronically on the lookout for pacifiers. Capitalism depends on it.

But Krank believes that attention can be fracked even more productively in the workplace—if stress is applied strategically. In fact, he claims that if people like Matt are well-managed, eventually they should be able to extract double the output for half the input.

Oh crap. Does this mean they'll be able to call a worker defective if he can't double his output?

You said it, Bubba, not me.

Oh. Oh. *And if they can call a worker defective, they have grounds to terminate with cause...*

Bingo. It's all about efficient fracking, my friend. Imagine some poor sod who has a thousand emails to face before he can even start his day—not to mention the system upgrades he has to master every month. Let's say he's a tidy guy; he likes things neat. He wants to know he's done by the end of the day and it kills him that he can never catch up. Still, he keeps on trying. Every day, one more bit of bandwidth per second... The subject, as they say, is ripe.

Now add a little heat—a little more pressure, a few more tasks each day—and watch the fracking begin. Oh, the suspense! Will the pipelines hold as the pressure mounts, or will they burst? Now factor in all the variables: different personalities, different jobs, different responses to internal climate change. How much heat is too much heat? So much to learn, so little time. Because we can be sure that the rest of the West is climbing on board just as fast as we are. We're all lab rats, kiddo. *Ha*—if we're "lucky."

Man, you're killing me here! Stop, already! What about the ones who frack and fry? Have they found a cure? Are they even looking?

Not that I know of. Realistically, why would they? Besides, the only way out of the causal mindset—the imperative to keep up with technology—is to abandon the imperative to keep up with technology. Which is like saying the only way to end war is to give up your nukes. Great idea, but hard to do when everyone else is stockpiling. And not exactly up there on the corporate to-do list.

Nobody wants to drop out or come last—inside the Depot or out. So unless you jump off a bridge or join a monastery, every solution just perpetuates the problem. You start using smart pills so you can go faster, but so does everyone else. You double the dosage, but so does everyone else. You need something to counter the side effects, but blah-blah-blah. And Big Pharma is always ten moves ahead—the next solutions are already packaged and on the shelves.

Speaking of which, I hear they're trying the latest bandwidth-booster—BB Gen3—on Matt right now. Simple daily injections, apparently, and no outrageous side effects (so far). They say it hits your system like really smooth crystal meth. The Depot was way overstocked before it hit the market, but now they can't keep up.

***

MATT?

MATT.

WE CAN SEE YOU, MATT. WE KNOW YOU ARE IN THE DISPENSARY. WE CAN SEE YOU STANDING BEHIND THE DOOR. YOU ARE VISIBLE ON SIX MONITORS, MATT. DO NOT PRETEND YOU ARE NOT THERE.

WE HAVE A SITUATION, MATT. WE NEED YOU TO TAKE A DOWN PILL. NOW. YOU HAVE JUST BURNED A WEEK'S WORTH OF BANDWIDTH TALKING TO AN IMAGINARY CO-WORKER.

YOU HAVE NO ONE WITH YOU, MATT. WHAT YOU HAVE IS A SERIOUS LEAK IN THE NORTHEAST LINE OF YOUR POSTERIOR TEMPORAL CORTEX. THE FRACKING HAS NOT BEEN 100% SUCCESSFUL THIS TIME.

YOU ARE HALLUCINATING, MATT. WE ARE HERE TO HELP.

IT'S TIME TO GO BACK TO YOUR UNIT, MATT. THE DOOR YOU ARE STANDING BEHIND WILL OPEN IN

EXACTLY FIVE SECONDS. PLEASE PUT THE NEEDLE DOWN AND PLACE THE BAGGIE BACK ON THE SHELF.

VERY GOOD, MATT. THAT'S VERY GOOD. WE ARE COMING IN NOW.

SOMETHING TO SAY

SOMETHING TO SAY

Erin Winter graded her last paper and glanced up at her five squirming captives. A whole hour wasted on an exam they would probably all bomb. An exam that should have been written in class a week ago—if they'd only bothered to show. And it had to be this day, when she'd organized the life out of it already.

Edward was coming for dinner. She rarely cooked on school nights, but tonight she had something to say. Something that couldn't wait.

She hated keeping students after class. The confinement was always worse for her. Edward said she was too soft; she should have just failed them. Maybe he was right.

She felt small and trapped behind her desk, intently grading papers with half a mind. Even the grading would have to be checked again.

Damn the waste.

Her watch, consulted for the hundredth time, at last read 4:00 o'clock. She braced herself and signalled a dismissal to the five miscreants, holding on through the noise and clatter they scattered in their wake.

A page fluttered up from her pile of papers as the last boy sprinted past. She lunged to retrieve it and missed, landing in a sprawl across her desk. She heaved herself part way up, then changed her mind and slumped back down, shoulders shaking in a mirthless chuckle. Her hair fell around her on the desk, dimming the harsh fluorescence of the room. The varnished wood felt cool on her cheek and she drifted for a moment, myopically scanning for omens in the scratches and stains.

"Toying with a new religion, Ms. Winter?" A bearded face appeared on the desk beside her. "Or better yet, a modern mating ritual? Head down, ass up, eyes closed, that sort of thing?"

"Jesus, Jack, when did you land?"

"But you landed me, sweet thing. A moment ago I was whistling home, a free man. Then zap! Snagged by an upturned ass and reeled in like a helpless halibut. Oh well, you got me now. Do your worst."

"Sorry pal." She heaved herself back to her seat with a crumpled grin. "Wrong culture. Wrong species too. Marine life three doors down—Mrs. Bollinger. Now buzz off and let me regroup."

"Hmm, do I detect a little crankiness? The prelude to an evening of ecstasy with the deadly Sir Eddie, perhaps?"

He ducked to miss her backhand and caught it squarely in the neck.

"*Ouch!* I was only teasing, for God's sake. You're coming to Crawley's first though, aren't you?"

She shook her head.

"Not even for one little half pint? Gabe's tending bar tonight; the whole gang will be there."

"Not tonight, Jack. I absolutely haven't got the time."

He sighed hugely and drifted off, pausing once to bash his head theatrically against the doorjamb.

In fact, there was nothing she'd rather do than join Gabe and the gang at Crawley's for a beer. Or several. It had been far too long.

What happened to all the fun? Where did that part of me go?

In a previous life, Erin had been a server at Crawley's herself, and Jack had been a regular for years. In fact, it was partly Jack's fault that she'd found herself teaching again. An opening had come up at his school and he'd started pestering her to look into it. He'd also told the principal that she was exceptionally qualified: "She not only has the credentials, she's also a server at my local bar—and trust me, anyone who can keep the peace at last call in a room full of drinking adults will find school kids a cakewalk."

Before she'd had a chance to process the idea, the job had landed in her lap.

* * *

Thinking back, being a server at Crawley's was the best job she'd ever had—more fun, more money, better exercise. Her friend Gabe was still there and she clearly still enjoyed it.

Erin and Gabe had met in a fifth-year education program at UBC, both having completed English degrees that didn't lead to gainful employment. A year later, both had learned that teaching high school English was stressful, all-consuming, and given the endless hours of marking and prep, ridiculously underpaid.

They'd met again by chance as servers at Crawley's, where the hours were flexible, the staff congenial, and the work finished when the shift ended. Erin had actually had time to write.

Why did I ever go back to teaching?

She knew why, though she didn't like to admit it. It wasn't only because Jack had made it so easy. It was also because Edward had openly assumed that bar work was something you did when you were going to school, or not qualified for anything else. She'd heard him say to friends that she was "really" a teacher... as if her regular presence at the bar was pure illusion.

The upshot was that for a muddle of reasons, she'd decided to give teaching another go.

Gabe had mentioned that an opening was coming up at Crawley's at the end of the year. Just two months away. She'd been trying to persuade Erin to apply.

"Think of it, Erin: You like the work, everyone knows you, and you can work part-time for the same money... maybe even get back to some writing."

It was a tempting thought, but there was no time to indulge it right now.

Where was I? She took a deep breath and wound up. *Okay—graded papers back in the pile, exams in the drawer, daybook and purse in the backpack...*

She cleared her desk, locked her drawer and scooped her coat and pack, donning them in stages as she zigzagged down the hall. Past the office, through the big double doors and outside. One blissful moment to stare into space before starting the car, then on to the market.

A thin rain was starting as she pulled into the mall. In the distance, a perfectly full moon floated between two tall trees. It was low in the sky and unusually bright through the late October drizzle.

Just in time for Halloween. *All I need is a hat and broom.*

Her mouth curled at the corners; becoming a witch would be just the thing right now. *Forget school, forget dinner, forget Edward. Just climb on your broom and fly to the moon.* (*Or maybe Paris.*) The thought was delicious.

She gazed at the moon and sighed. *If only I wasn't so bloody responsible...*

The hum of motion and muzak engulfed her as she glided down the aisles. Salad greens, rice and wine—done. A shudder as she found herself humming to *The Dreams of the Everyday*

Housewife. Then back to the car.

Home at last, she marched up the stairs to her second-floor apartment and shifted into high gear. With a practiced pirouette, she dropped the groceries, shuffled off her pack and shed her coat and boots. Retrieving the groceries, she continued down the hall to the kitchen. Casserole out of the fridge and into the oven. Rice rinsed and planted on the stove. Burners on. Time: 5:00 p.m.

Peeling off clothes, she proceeded to the bathroom and pulled a pair of tights from the towel rack. A five-minute warm-up, twenty minutes to work out and five to stretch. Bringing it to 5:30. Another ten minutes for a shower, and a final ten for the salad...

Leaving ten for a glass of wine before he arrives. Time to catch my breath and think things through.

Hurry up so you can slow down. Story of my life.

She was reminded of the family walks she'd had to endure as a child. More like marches, really—always too fast for short legs. She'd run ahead so she could stop and catch her breath, but they'd always show up before she'd had time.

She could still feel the ancient agitation in the hollow beneath her ribs.

Just find the right words. There must be a simple way to say it. Simple and clear and matter-of-fact. You have to say something. Tonight without fail.

Her mind raced, rehearsing phrases and discarding them like so many worn-out clothes. Nothing fit. This was underplayed, that was too dramatic. Why were there never words?

Okay, stop thinking and get on with it. Give yourself time to wind down. Hurry up so you can slow down. The words will come if you're not in a state.

From the street, a rapid series of explosions made her jump.

Firecrackers. They sounded so much like gunshots. Someone's kid had found the Halloween stash a day early; it happened every year. She made a mental note to buy sweets for the trick-or-treaters.

It occurred to her to call and ask Edward to come a little later. Just half an hour would do it; she could tell him she'd been detained. But the prospect only increased her agitation. There'd be an interrogation. He'd want to know why she'd wasted time keeping kids after school, and it wouldn't sound reasonable after the fact.

The thing was, it had simply been expedient because all five kids had come to class today. Which was rare. She imagined explaining to Edward that his dinner would be late because she'd wanted to give five kids one more chance at their mid-term exam. Because she hadn't wanted to fail them just for failing to show. Because they were messed-up, hormone-driven teenagers and despite her agitation, she was actually very fond of them...

No. Too many reasons. One had to say this kind of thing with simple authority. And no explanations.

She finished her workout, stretched and showered, wondering all the while what Edward would have done in her place. He wasn't a cruel person; surely he would have felt some compassion for the little monsters too.

She'd been quite smitten with Edward at first. Finally, she'd thought, someone reasonably normal. Intelligent, apparently stable and not chronically broke. A software engineer with an IT firm. Well-respected and clearly solvent.

He was a charmer too. He'd brought her flowers on their first date. He held her chair in restaurants and occasionally opened her car door. He complimented her when she dressed up. He was old-fashioned and sweet in those ways.

He was also nice looking, and he dressed well. She liked looking at him. He was studious, if somewhat confused, in bed. But then, who wasn't?

For a time she'd believed she was really in love with him, and that had felt wonderful. But after a few months, it had gone flat. *What was it?*

It had taken a while to nail it because it wasn't overt. It was not what he said or did, though there were issues there too. It was more that she couldn't find him. Beyond the pleasing surface and the mental acuity, she couldn't detect his essential flavour—the music and texture of his being.

Perhaps it was just too different from her own. Whatever the case, she'd begun to feel increasingly lonely in his presence.

He read voraciously and could argue all the finer points of geopolitics, but nothing seemed to move him. Or bruise him. He seemed as impervious to the tender blue of the evening sky as he was to the horrors of climate change.

Not that one required people to be pervious all the time—God forbid—but it was disconcerting. And he didn't listen to music either. She'd been stunned to discover that he didn't even own a sound system. When asked, he'd explained that he didn't dislike music itself, he just didn't like what it did to him. "I find it intrusive. Controlling. It stains my brain and changes my mood. Leaves traces that last all day..."

Not that everyone had to listen to music. And she understood about the traces.

He found certain courtesies controlling as well. If he was on foot, waiting to cross the street, for example, and the driver of a car waved him on, he'd be irritated. "That was not his call," he'd say. "I had clearly stopped to indicate that I was waiting for him. He had no business overriding my call..."

The disdain was also not helpful. He'd resort to mockery when he was out of his depth. Or sarcasm. They were crude defenses and Erin had tried to be understanding. But he didn't seem to realize that he wounded people. He seemed incapable of remorse.

For a time she'd told herself that she was being too fussy; she needed to accept the bad with the good; maybe this was as good as it got, etc., etc.

That time had passed. It was the loneliness. It was all too pointless and sad.

You must simply say that the whole thing has gone dead and it has to end.

From nowhere, tears. An involuntary river streaming down her cheeks.

For Christ's sake, woman, put the lid on! There'll be time for sadness later.

It wasn't just sadness though; it was the immensity of the task ahead.

You're tired and overwhelmed, that's all. But you must not run out of steam. Not tonight.

Time: 5:45 p.m.

Okay, still time for a glass of wine. Dress, touch up your face, check on dinner. Save the salad till he's here; it won't take long. There should be ten minutes.

Alas, not. Two sharp knocks on the door, the sound of a key.

Crap! Early? Are you serious?

He entered without a greeting. Greetings were apparently clichés. Her throat closed.

My face. Dammit.

Her eyes in the mirror were red-rimmed and puffy.

Lid on, Erin. Kill it. Do not be emotional.

She threw cold water at her face and pinched her cheeks to make the red more uniform. She breathed in, then out, then opened the door a crack and called out.

"I'm in the bathroom, Edward. Come in and sit down, I'll be right out."

Her voice was not quite right. He wandered down the hall to the bathroom and looked in. Cocking his head to one side, he arched an eyebrow, looked her up and down and nodded twice. Then he bowed back out and closed the door.

The intrusion was brisk and strangely anaesthetizing. At once her face composed itself and her body relaxed. Without effort or conscious thought, the lid went softly down.

It was an awesome transformation. The man worked miracles.

She went to meet him with lightness and air—not sweet, not sad, not warm, not cold. Not personal. It was lovely.

They fell into their easy ritual of lightweight murmurings. Casual chat that cooled the air, declaring peace. Erin brought him wine, perched briefly on the arm of his chair and inquired after his day.

A few minutes later she went to the kitchen, leaving him with his *Globe and Mail.* She felt lightheaded and oddly reprieved, suspended in a beautiful vacuum of non-feeling. It was pleasant. It was peaceful and comfortable, and somehow he was responsible. She felt warmly toward him. She genuinely felt like pleasing him.

She began to hum as she started the salad, smiling to herself for no reason. An old Paul Simon song was circling her brain... How did it go?

Just slip out the back, Jack
Make a new plan, Stan
You don't need to be coy, Roy
Just get yourself free...

She chuckled quietly to herself. She felt a little giddy, as if she'd passed a test by sheer fluke and no one else knew. There was comfort in the secret. And power. For some odd reason, it was also very funny. A large hoot was dying to escape.

She stifled a snicker as she began to chop, then held her breath, listening for sounds of investigation.

Nothing. Just the faint rustle of his paper as he turned a page.

She breathed out, shuddering to arrest a fresh wave of giggles.

Her mind strayed back to her earlier resolve. She was to say something tonight. Really say something, without fail.

She picked up a tomato and resumed chopping.

Not yet though. It wouldn't sound right when things are so nice. After dinner, when we're sitting with a coffee and brandy. I'll be matter-of-fact. No whining, no blaming. I'll simply explain that the thing has to stop. The problem is...

The problem was that Edward had a knack for making her feel like an idiot when she tried to discuss their relationship. He'd tell her she was a hopeless idealist, never satisfied, couldn't see a good thing when she was standing in the middle of it...

"We're perfect," he'd say. "We work brilliantly. We were made for each other and deep down you know it. Why are you always trying to fix things that aren't broken...?"

It was the case-closed tone. He'd make her feel like her compass was cracked—again.

You will not let him do it this time... He needs to see that it can't go on. He must feel it too, the deadness and the loneliness. I can't be the only one...

The lump returned to her throat and a splash sounded loudly on the back of her hand. She swallowed hard and swiped at her eyes.

For God's sake, not now. This is not the time. Get on with it. Finish the bloody salad.

She shook her head and forced herself back to the task at hand. As if possessed, her hands took on a life of their own. Seeds and stems, leaves and stalks flew into the bowl as she willed herself back to the peaceful vacuum of non-feeling.

Then suddenly she stopped. Something in the blur of her vision was wrong. A loud crimson was screaming from the green of the bowl. She reached uneasily to touch it and quickly retracted her hand. It was warm and sticky and it ran through her fingers as she tried to lift it out. She swiped at her face to clear her eyes, leaving a trail of red down one cheek. Then she pulled back her hair, unable to register.

She stared at her hand, marvelling that she'd felt nothing. She still felt nothing. She could see where she'd sliced through the fleshy mound at the base of her palm. Blood rushed from a deep gash, spilling over her wrist and down her arm.

Crap, Erin! You've made a bloody mess!

She looked more closely. It was a gusher, but she knew first aid and could see that the gash was a safe distance from the radial artery. She'd probably need a few stitches—inconvenient, but not life-threatening.

I can not *believe this. Not tonight of all nights.*

She tried to arrest the flood with paper towels, but couldn't see because her hair was in the way. Forgetting the bloody hand, she pulled it back, leaving fresh streaks of red.

The whole thing was becoming ridiculous.

Not exactly part of the plan, Erin—ha!

It was too hysterical. Really.

A wave of insane laughter threatened to break. She held her sides to contain it, causing a fresh gush to bloody the front of her shirt. This sent her over the top. It was like being in one of those zany cartoons where every attempt at coming unstuck just gets you stickier. Through a strangled cackle, she told herself to get a grip.

I mean—could I have botched this more perfectly if I'd tried?

She thought of calling Edward, but couldn't bear the thought of his what-now frown.

Her face and hair were now stiffening on the parts that were smeared, which were rapidly forming crusts. Her whole top was smeared as well, and both sleeves soaked.

She wanted to scream, "Edward, come quickly!" but couldn't. It would sound so pathetic. Besides, she couldn't let him see her like this. Not tonight of all nights. She could already see the irritation on his face. And the self-effacing smile on her own. She hated that smile.

She pressed a fresh towel against the cut and leaned against the counter to gather her wits. What was the formula here? What did one do when one was a bloody mess in the kitchen, planning to feed and break up with the man in the living room? Who was completely unaware of either the blood or the plan...?

She drew a blank.

On impulse, she lifted the towel and watched as the blood gushed freshly from the cut. The force of it was fascinating, the colour gorgeous.

The colour of life. My life. Spilling, bubbling, breaking free.

There was something joyful about it. All that life breaking free from all that life. Really, it was all she wanted. Just to break free. She realized she could actually make it happen if she wanted to. Quite easily, in fact. Just a slightly deeper cut at a slightly different angle...

It was tempting in an abstract way, the thought of complete cessation. Drifting off to the lovely vacuum of non-feeling. Inviting, for a moment. She'd occasionally had fantasies of driving off a cliff. Or of Edward driving off a cliff—accidentally of course. Breaking free, one way or another. So much simpler than breaking up.

A second explosion of firecrackers jolted her out of her reverie. She thought again of Halloween.

Better to fly to the moon on a broom. (Or Paris.)

The thing was, she only really craved cessation when she was with Edward. Sadness and loneliness were different when she was on her own. She didn't really mind them at all.

Back to business.

It was time to assess the damage, clean up and get on with dinner. She put a fresh towel around the cut and went to the bathroom to have a look.

She was utterly unprepared for what she saw.

It was horrifying. It was spectacular. It was completely disorienting.

She steadied herself and took a breath, then looked more closely. Her sleeves were heavy with crusted blood, her face was a stiff red smirk, and her hair sported wild red streaks on both sides. They stuck out in sinister spokes and waggled like giant spider legs when she moved her head. She could see no trace of her familiar self.

It was like looking at a freshly fed vampire.

Even better than a witch. Remarkable, really. One last detail would do it...

She couldn't resist. Lifting her arm to her mouth, she sucked gently on a sleeve, then bared her bloody teeth.

It was brilliant. She was no longer Erin Winter. She was the Queen of Halloween.

As she played with various faces, she thought of the masquerade balls of old. She'd never realized how liberating a change of costume could be. How effortlessly a person could shift from a Jekyll to a Hyde...

A new game plan was forming. It was insane. It was good. It would require a totally straight face and a no-nonsense tone. She would have to own the part completely.

She wound a clean cloth around her hand, winked at the mirror and took a deep breath. Then she strode into the living room.

"Edward," she said, "Listen, please; I have something to say. The thing is, I have some unusual appetites that don't get fed in this relationship. So I'm afraid you and I are done. Oh, and dinner's off too—sorry about that."

Edward gasped and jumped to his feet. "What are you *talking* about? My *God*, what have you *done* to yourself??"

She sucked gently on a sleeve and gave him a bloody smile. Which knocked him back into his seat.

"Nothing to get in a twist about, Edward. It's just a now and again thing. You know, when the moon is full and all that. Mainly cats lately—the little rascals can be feisty, as you can see. But the thing is, appetites do change from time to time, and I thought you should know. In any event, I have things to do now, so please run along."

He choked. He froze. He spluttered. He looked wildly around the room. The furniture looked settled and peaceful. The goblins, if they were home, were clearly content to hide in the woodwork. Everything but Erin looked perfectly normal.

"This is preposterous!" he shouted. "What are you playing at? This is not happening!"

He wanted to be outraged. Offended. Appalled. Anything. But there was no slot in his brain to park it all. No well-worn groove for a clear-cut reaction. Sarcasm had nowhere to land and mockery seemed ill-advised.

Bereft of his usual responses, he grew increasingly jumpy. For a long moment, he stared at his feet.

When he looked up again, a small involuntary squeak escaped from the back of his nose. Erin suppressed a snort, then summoned what she hoped was a sympathetic smile.

It was not. All Edward saw was a murderous smirk.

Mortified now, he stuffed his belongings into his pack, threw the door key at the coffee table and raced out.

As he sped down the stairs, Erin stepped onto the landing.

"Only fooling, Eddie!" she called in a loud whisper.

He didn't hear. Or if he did, he didn't turn around. *All for the best*, she thought. There would be time for explanations another day. Or not.

She went back inside, cleaned up and called a cab. Five stitches later, she cabbed home again and called Gabe to say she would like to apply for the opening at Crawley's. They made plans to celebrate later in the week and rang off.

She turned the oven back on, donned a rubber glove and dressed the salad. As she set the table for one, she found herself humming again:

Just hop on the bus, Gus
You don't need to discuss much
Drop off the key, Lee
And get yourself free...

Then she sat down to eat. She could already feel a story brewing.

STEPPING OUT

STEPPING OUT

—PRAEAMBULUS—

Who are they all, Fredrik?
Who?
You know, the voices.
Oh. Just me.
All of them?
Yes.
Even the ones in the furniture?
Yes.
Even the beetle?
Of course. You know beetles can't talk.
But where did they come from?
The Stork.
Come on.
Okay. God.
Tsk, I hate when you do that... Hey! What about me?
What about you?
Am I you too?
Of course.
Crap. Does that mean I get kicked out in the end?
Nah. I think I'll keep you around, just to annoy me.

Okay, so who put the yellow Post-it on the bathroom mirror?

The beetle's uncle.

You're really not going to tell me, are you?

You're really not going to believe me, are you? Okay, how about this? You're all just pathetic little splinters of my fractured little psyche, trying like mad to run away from home (or pester me to death) before the whole rickety show blows up. As in, *projections.*

I thought so.

No you didn't.

Yes I did.

No. You didn't. Or you wouldn't have asked.

I was just checking.

No you weren't.

Yes I was.

No. You. Were. *Not.*

(*You just make stuff up, Fredrik.*)

(Right. And you don't, I suppose.)

STEPPING OUT

—AMBULUS PRIMARIUS—

You could use a little help, amigo.

"Blue ink on a faded yellow Post-it, stuck to the bathroom mirror. The Post-it on a tilt, curling slightly inward. The words slanting downward to the right, suggesting (from a distance, without glasses) a hand extended shyly to be kissed."

Or limply to be shaken.

Shyly kissed, limply shaken; it could go either way.

Or a helping hand.

It could go *many* ways. The point being, words that are asking to be noticed. Attention-seeking words.

Me words.

Written, apparently, in the royal hand.

We words.

A paradox.

A poser.

Pointless to ponder. On to Serious Matters of State. A little fanfare here, I think.

Righto. Hear ye! Hear ye! Make way for the splashing of the royal face! Make way for the combing of the royal hair! Make way for the descent of the royal personage down the royal stairs! Make way for the placement of the royal bottom on the royal chair!

You could use a little help, amigo.

STOP THIS NONSENSE. GET STARTED. TELL ABOUT FREDRIK. THIRD PERSON.

Right. Let's get on with it.

Wait a minute—who was that?

Who?

The bossy one, in the capitals. Where did he come from?

Just a splinter, like the rest. He gives the orders and keeps the story straight.

What story?

The bit in quotations, dumb-ass. Now shut up and let me get on with it.

Right. Let's get on with it.

"As he spooned out coffee, spikey snatches of late-night resolutions made ineffectual stabs at the knot in Fredrik's brain."

Spikey snatches? Ineffectual stabs?

Okay, "sharp shards, dot-dot-dot, futile strikes, dot-dot-dot."

Sharp shards made futile strikes at the knot in Fredrik's brain? Jesus.

That's right—sharp shards made futile strikes. As they were wont to do.

Wont?

Wont.

As in "wont, wonted, wonting?"

As in wont.

As in "I wont what I wont when I wont it?"

As in fuck off.

Cowboy.

Are you quite done? Should I walk around the block a few times?

Okay, okay. Resolutions. What resolutions?

For God's sake, where do you go at night?

STOP DRAGGING YOUR FEET. TELL ABOUT FREDRIK. STICK TO THIRD PERSON.

Right, thank you.

"Resolutions to do with last resorts. Fredrik's train of thought had been derailed, he now recalled, by the initially enlightening but ultimately mind-blowing effects of a bottle of Mortlach Rare."

The last and best of Dee-Dee's Scotch. Har-de-har.

"Not being much of a drinker, he estimated it would take him most of the day to recover."

No regrets, though. No regrets.

"By the second piece of toast, the knot in his brain had eased enough to permit whole thoughts. Resolutions, he concluded, were the wily spawn of altered states. Shifty, unpredictable creatures. Marginally appealing to a damaged brain at 3:00 in the morning; hopeless companions after dawn."

Bravo.
Merci.

"Resolutions to do with last resorts were particularly bothersome. Far too many unknowns. The challenge of deciding what qualified, for starters. And if that became a known—which it never did—the challenge of deciding when to exercise one. Was there an indicator of some kind? Did one see the deep end approaching in time to ready one's ducks? Or was it more usual to fall in and flail about for a time first?"

My money's on the falling and flailing.

"The word *last* was problematic, implying as it did that others came before. The problem was, how many? If you didn't know how many items were in a series, how could you know when you'd got to the last one?"

Always the numbers man, our Fredrik. Always the crazy mathematician.

"Which brought up questions of order: What determined sequence in a series of resorts? Fredrik had always assumed that therapy would come last, but when you got right down to it, there were no logical grounds for the assumption. Besides, he'd tried therapy once. The man had asked him to write an autobiography for the second visit—daunting assignment—and he hadn't come to the end of it yet."

How could he? He was still alive. Things were still happening.

"And then there was God. Or was there? Was God a viable option or just a sneaky way to hedge one's bets? By what standards did one measure merit in such matters? It felt vaguely disloyal to exclude Him and completely ridiculous not to."

Dear old God. He reminds me of Uncle Ivan.
What—the long hair? The beard?
No no—the early retirement; the regrets.
Oh. Right.

"The thing had a way of spiralling out. Without guidelines for sequence or merit, it seemed irresponsible to assume that God or therapy were even in the running. Still, he'd find himself rehearsing with an imaginary therapist as he foraged for dinner..."

(Mealtimes could be wontsome.)

"'I guess it started shortly after mother's death...' He'd picture the encouraging nod.

"'*Ah. So you have been feeling pushed around by things since your mother died, have I got that right? You say household objects have been harassing you. Your furniture in particular has taken on a—hrm—bullying tone.*'

"Fredrik would snort; then he'd laugh out loud. The trouble was, he'd want the therapist to laugh out loud too. He'd want them both to have a good chuckle and dismiss the whole thing as—well, just one of those things. A passing nuisance."

A fleeting thing. As in temporary, or short-lived. Possessing the quality of ephemerality or brevity. As in transitory. Characterized by impermanence. A Zen-ish thing...
Shut up.

"It was true the nuisance had coincided with Dee-Dee's death, but so far Fredrik had felt no more bereft than he might at the loss of a vaguely onerous job. It could as easily be a mid-life thing, or the result of some innocuous conversation overheard in a bar. It might not be traceable to anything at all."

> *A causeless thing, possessing the quality of randomness; a thing without origin...*

"Hoping a stray recollection might yield a clue, he decided to give the biography a try."

Biography: Fredrik Johann Swanson
Entry # 1, February 2

Fredrik Johann Swanson

- Age: sixty-five
- Only child of Deirdre-Dawne (Dee-Dee) Swanson and Johann Tomas Swanson

Factors of possible significance:

- Father:
    - — Born Johann Tomas Svendsen; immigrated from Norway to Canada after WW 2
    - — Changed name to Swanson on becoming a Canadian citizen
    - — Died at sea at forty-six (complications from food poisoning)—I was eleven
    - — Health Problems: none that I knew of; mother said he was depressive

- Occupation: chief officer on Norwegian freighter; away a lot, home a lot
- Financial Status: "comfortable"
- Habits, Hobbies: smoked a pipe; paced outside deck or living room floor, enjoyed walking, puttering in workshop, reading biographies, arguing politics
- Personality: formal; disliked small-talk; angry when embarrassed
- Relationship with father: formal
- Special Memories: tried to teach me facts of life—uncomfortable; took me fishing once—also uncomfortable (did not catch anything)

• Mother:

- Died in her sleep at ninety-two, eight months ago. Cause of death: heart attack. (Death not surprising, given age, cigarettes, Scotch, etc. Still, came as a bit of a shock)
- Health Problems: cataracts and broken hip in her eighties; otherwise healthy
- Occupation: mother, housewife, realtor
- Financial Status: wealthy; inherited modest fortune at father's death (life insurance); quadrupled same through buying and selling real estate
- Personality: charming, flamboyant, adamant (about everything), aggressively warm, seamlessly narcissistic
- Hobbies, Habits: lived for amateur theatre; loved performing—always on stage

— Relationship with mother—informal, unpredictable, dramatic, exhausting
— Special Memories—nothing stands out; everything stands out

This is pointless.

YOU HAVE BARELY STARTED. TELL ABOUT LIFE WITH DEE-DEE.

Really, it's pointless.

JUST DO IT. THIRD PERSON.

"When the hip had happened ten years earlier—a fall while playing a spirited, if over-ripe Kate in *The Taming of the Shrew*—Fredrik had come back to Kitsilano to help out. His marriage had just ended and he was temporarily homeless, so the return to Highbury Street had for a time been both a convenience and a distraction."

Okay, so right here is why Fredrik can't do therapy. You can hear the man already...
"Ah. So your marriage ended and you moved back in with your mother. And how did that work out for you?"
Seriously—just mention a person moving in with his mother, and... Well, you heard the tone.

COME ON, PUSH THROUGH.

I hate this.

"Once his mother was mobile again, they settled in to their own routines. She occupied the main floor of the house and Fredrik took over the upstairs. He left the bathroom and one of the two back bedrooms as they were, converting the second bedroom into a kitchen with an outside entrance and stairs to the street. He opened the two front rooms to make one large space looking north over the harbour. On the right walking in was his study, on the left, his living room, and lining the inside walls, his library. All in all, he was quite self-contained."

> Okay, so now he sounds like he's trying to prove his independence. As soon as there's a therapist in the room, people start trying to prove their independence. You know what they call that? Over-compensation. That's what they'll say Fredrik has. A case of over-compensation.

NEVER MIND. KEEP GOING.

"Conveniently, the only requirement for his work with the Naples Institute was access to the web. Not so conveniently, the Institute had lost funding since merging with the university. Contracts for independent mathematicians were currently scarce."

> You can hear what's coming, right?
> *"Ah. So you lost not only your mother but your work as well..."*
> Can you see him connecting the dots? He's going to tell Fredrik he has loss issues. Mention a man losing his work and his mother and right away he has loss issues. Just wait till we get to Pamela.

TALK ABOUT PAMELA THEN. USE THE BIO.

Sure, why not? Let's get Fredrik all wrapped up in time for lunch.

Bio—FJS—March 28

Pamela:

— Woman I was dating for four years (till three months ago)
— Occupation: ocular medical technician
— How We Met: she advised us on post-surgery care after mother's cataracts; two professional visits, one chance meeting at Granville Island, went for coffee, etc.
— Personality: introverted, competent, straight-ahead, not given to dramatic outbursts
— Habits, Hobbies: walking, curling, crosswords, movies; collecting things; organizing things; cleaning things
— Mother's Response: loved being part of our meeting; found Pamela bland. (Of note: Dee-Dee found everyone but Dee-Dee bland.)
— Also of Note: fact that I was conducting my private life on the floor above hers was a matter of pride for Dee-Dee. She believed it proved she was a modern woman.

"Ah. And I imagine it kept you conveniently at her beck and call as well?"

I can't keep doing this with him doing that. Did you notice the tone this time?

TELL ABOUT AFTER DEE-DEE DIED.

Right.

"It was now eight months since Dee-Dee's death, and Fredrik was going through a rough patch. He was feeling pushed around by things. Objects had begun to pester him.

"He'd felt little in the way of grief, and though he knew that delayed reactions were not uncommon, he did not feel like he'd been keeping anything at bay. In fact, he'd felt quite euphoric in those first few weeks and months. So many oppressive rituals had evaporated overnight. Small things, like always having dinner in the dining room. Always doing the dishes right afterward. Laundry on Monday nights, CBC radio in the mornings.

"For the first while, he took a childish pleasure in neglecting them all. He let the dishes pile up, he ignored the laundry, he forgot to shave. He ate his dinner in the kitchen, or ignored mealtimes altogether, grazing at odd hours in front of the fridge. He skipped his morning showers.

"The feeling of space was exhilarating; he had the whole house to himself. A hundred possibilities presented themselves. He could stay up all night if he wished. He could refuse to answer the phone or door. He could invite strange and interesting people to drop by. He could invite strange and interesting women to lunch...

"At this, Fredrik would think of Pamela and feel guilty. Patient Pamela, who had been waiting as long as he had, or so it seemed, for things to be different. There was an understanding that if it weren't for Dee-Dee, they'd have more time together, more intimacy, a chance to travel. Definitely better sex.

"Pamela had been a welcome relief after the neurotic intensity of his wife, but with Dee-Dee gone, their relationship had felt oddly hollow. Perhaps this was natural, given that it was through Dee-Dee they'd come together, and on Dee-Dee's turf they'd spent most of their time. The winks as they listened to her endless diatribes, the nods as they made their escapes after dinner, all bespoke a mediated intimacy, dependent for its existence on an outside element. With Dee-Dee gone, their relationship was characterized more by the absence of a bonding force than the presence of a forceful bond."

> *(Psst. Nobody talks like that.)*
> Dammit. Nobody talks like that. This third person business isn't working. Everything sounds all linear and narratory. The words are too stiff.
> *It's Fredrik who's too stiff. Fredrik makes the words go stiff.*
> Fredrik is not stiff. He's a bit formal, that's all.
> *Fredrik is stiff as a board. And neurotic. And obsessive.*
> He is not. He's just a bit reserved.
> *Actually, Fredrik is downright prim. He might as well be wearing lace doilies.*

STOP IT. GO ON NOW. TELL ABOUT THE FURNITURE THING.

> Sure, throw me in the deep end.
> *Throw me in the end with the most depth. Throw me in the end with the least shallowness. Throw me in the end with the... something.*
> Ha.

YOU'RE STALLING. GET ON WITH IT.

> Right.
> *(...most vertical extension.)*

"Then there was the thing with the furniture. It was a background thing at first, situated in one of those anaemic little pockets of the mind where sixties songs lived out their stale existences. Just part of the general din.

"Over time though, perhaps because of its novelty, the phenomenon had moved from the background to the foreground of Fredrik's mind. Objects had begun to take on personalities. Demanding, disapproving personalities for the most part.

"At first it was idle entertainment. Fredrik indulged it in the same spirit that he indulged the little mechanisms that made rhymes, or counted things, or turned words into meaningless purees of sound by repeating them to death."

(But hey, nothing neurotic about our Fredrik.)

"It started one morning as he was walking through the living room to fetch his paper. He bent down to pick up a wood chip and when he stood up again, he noticed that the room looked suddenly unfamiliar. It made him think of a stage setting—an elaborate stage that exuded such a powerful mixture of pretence and expectation, he was momentarily transfixed.

"He looked more intently. How had he not seen it before? The careful choreography, the suspension: the armchairs and sofa in their perfect semi-circle around the fire, patiently awaiting their passengers. The lamps waiting to offer their cozy glow. The paintings waiting to be admired. Everything waiting for the congenial gathering that was clearly not about to happen.

"'*Well?*' they all seemed to be saying.

"It was not a room that suggested a single dweller, let alone a recluse. It was a room that fairly blared bonhomie. The sofas and armchairs especially: all those open arms and empty laps. The obvious expectation; the disappointment waiting to happen. And beneath it, the *tone*. Critical, disapproving. A trace of mockery. The faint, yet distinct implication that someone was not measuring up.

"Fredrik started going the long way round to fetch his paper. It soon made no difference, however, for once it had his attention, the thing quickly spread to infect the whole main floor of the house. It was fascinating how seductive a new perception could be. And how difficult to suppress. As difficult as suppressing a yawn. Or trying to not think of a white elephant.

"Try to look at an object and not see what the object expects of you. A floor says, '*Walk on me;*' a door says, '*Open me;*' a table says, '*Eat here.*'"

Easier to not think of a white elephant.

Exactly.

"In a short while, the thing had become oppressive. Wherever there were objects, there were expectations—vocal now, and increasingly aggressive. The chair in the entry made petulant appeals as Fredrik walked in the door: '*Sit on me! Sit on meee!*' Then sulked when he failed to comply. The dining room table glared disapprovingly under its layer of dust. The bulging mailbox fizzed.

"Fredrik felt harassed. He then felt silly for feeling harassed, then resentful for feeling silly. And behind it all was the niggling fear that the thing might escalate.

"Though he sensed it was foolhardy—knowing as well as the next person that objects can neither speak nor listen, really—his first reaction on being accosted was to talk back. He quickly discovered that this only made things worse.

"If he told the armchair, 'I'm busy right now,' the chair would reply with an insult or a challenge...

"'*Woo, Mr. Big-Shot's a busy boy. What's he so busy about that he can't sit down for two little minutes in a comfortable chair? Is he busy stopping a war? Is he busy saving a rain forest? No wait—let me guess! He's busy going to the kitchen to make lunch!'*

"Then it would cackle hysterically till Fredrik was out of range.

"His second strategy was a pre-emptive strike. The moment he heard the first stirrings of an attack, he would tell the object to get lost. 'Fuck off!' he would shout. 'Fuck right off and stay fucked off!' This worked briefly, but soon he was hearing sarcastic little echoes in response:

"'Fuck off!' he says. 'Fuck right off and stay fucked off!' Mr. Big-Shot's swearing at the furniture now. And he can't even swear right. Nobody says 'stay fucked off.' Ha-ha!'

"If he tried ignoring them, they'd attack him for that:

"'Oh, now he's ignoring us. He thinks if he ignores us we won't exist. He thinks we'll go away. As if an armchair and a table could just get up and walk out the door...'

"He finally resorted to distracting himself till the object in question was out of range. To avoid the dining room table, he'd start a conversation with the kitchen stove. To avoid further contact with the stove, he'd start a new conversation with the fridge. When too many objects accosted him at once, he'd start singing something loud and snappy. The strategy worked to some degree, but it was labour-intensive. It irritated Fredrik that his newfound spaciousness was becoming so unaccountably cluttered."

> *(We should perhaps emphasize that there was nothing neurotic going on here. We should perhaps remind ourselves that our Fredrik was Mister Perfectly Normal.)*
>
> (Fuck off.)
>
> *(And stay fucked off?)*
>
> (Yes.)

STOP IT. TELL ABOUT THE POT.

"It was soon apparent that the object-harassment had a control centre, which took the form of the ceramic pot that lived on the dining room table. The pot had squatted on its four short paws like a bloated toad in the middle of its shiny oak pond for as long as Fredrik could remember. Despite the splashes of pink on its mud-green bulk and the flowers it was filled with from time to time, its bearing was invariably sinister. It would stir ever so slightly when Fredrik walked by.

"The pot had been Dee-Dee's pride and joy, her one and only artistic creation. In perverse moments, Fredrik had seen it as a kind of rival sibling—the only other survivor of his mother's ovens."

(Oh, gross.)

"He had always hated it, and the only thing that had so far kept him from throwing it away was the insane notion that she would find out. And be furious. Though he knew this was mad, he didn't have the nerve to override it. And the pot seemed to know it."

(Pots are amazingly clairvoyant. Little-known fact.)
(Shut up.)

TELL ABOUT THE EMPTY SPACES.

"The blank white walls and smooth white tiles of the kitchen were a welcome sight after passing the pot. Empty spaces offered a semblance of peace, though they were also potentially dangerous. One could fall into them and disappear. Fredrik had lost time gazing at the kitchen floor.

"There was a strange allure to emptiness, a seductive pull

that beckoned him, despite his habitual reserve. Since Dee-Dee's death, he had lived too much in the choppy waters of incessant activity. He wanted to come to a stop. Apart from the settling of the estate and the furniture thing, there had been far too much family activity. Aunts and uncles and bluff, hearty cousins had been coming out of the woodwork, all wanting to help.

"He'd tried to be polite. They were not a bad lot, and he did not want to appear ungrateful. But he felt thinned out in family gatherings. The conversations left him hungry. He was bored to tears by the sketchy reports: who was having children, who was getting rich, who was graduating or being promoted. He chafed against the dull constraints of topical respectability. No one, it seemed, was expected to talk beyond the headlines of things. And yet, despite the topical blandness, the same frothy fervour would prevail in every conversation.

"Fredrik would participate in a lurchy, on-again off-again fashion. Occasionally he'd get hooked by the fact that he knew a thing or two about the subject. His heart would beat faster as he waited his turn to speak, but invariably by the time there was an opening, the conversation would have moved on. He'd madly retreat in mid-sentence as all eyes turned at first encouragingly toward him, then nervously away.

"He'd make an excuse to leave early and come home exhausted."

Bio—FJS, April 7

- — I will never be social again. It is hectic and embarrassing and noisy.
- — I want the opposite.
- — I want the big background emptiness behind all the noise.

— I want to sink back to where it's quiet.

(He wants to hit "Select All" and "Delete.")
(He does not. And what if he did.)

Bio—FJS, April 7, cont'd.

— What does the hamster do when he jumps off the wheel?
— Where does he go when the cage door opens?
— Does he wander into a bigger cage or does he fall off the edge of the world?

(Hang on—where did the hamster come from?)
(It's a metaphor.)
(Are you serious? A hamster is the best you can do??)
(Shut up. Forget the hamster.)

"There had to be more to life. Certainly there had to be more than the incessant chewing of his overactive mind, which turned every thought into the same stale wad of flavourless gum and left a hollow where something substantial was supposed to land.

"Emptiness beckoned, but it also warned. It crouched in the background and breathed on the back of Fredrik's neck.

"Fredrik resisted it. He knew that a line could be crossed. He might be gone, just like that, without even knowing it. The prospect was only a little worse than the prospect of things remaining the same. But it *was* worse. It conjured up images of walking the streets naked, singing bad opera. Anything could happen. How would he know? He'd be gone—swallowed alive by whatever was breathing back there.

"He concluded that the thing to do with emptiness was to keep it in the background. In fact, he began to realize that most of his problems arose when the background and foreground of things got mixed up. Witness the furniture situation. At first it was just an amusing tic, one among many in the cluttered backyard of his overactive mind. But he had indulged it. He had allowed it to come to the foreground, and now look at the mess he was in. The thing was to keep things in their place."

(But in a laid-back way, right? Not in a neurotic-obsessive way.)
(Drop dead.)

FINISH TELLING ABOUT PAMELA.

"All very easy to say. If keeping things in their place was a chore on the home front, it was soon to become a colossal challenge around Pamela. When the object harassment had first begun, it had confined itself to inanimate objects. Visits from Pamela had actually normalized things. But lately things had been taking a different turn.

"For one thing, Fredrik was still between contracts with the Italians. It would be at least a month before he received his next assignment, and with nothing for his mind to chew on and no more directives from his mother, he was in graver danger than ever of falling into space.

"Having spent the last two years on a complicated logic problem, he was used to being mentally submerged. He no longer needed the money, but his mind still needed problems to solve, and despite the fact that he read voraciously, tackled several crosswords a day and puttered in the garden, the nagging feeling that background was creeping into foreground persisted. Reading, crosswords and puttering were meant to be fillers, not staples.

"Into this crucible would step the solicitous Pamela, a little less confident than she'd been before things 'got different.' Though it was something of a shock to see Fredrik unshaven and dishevelled one day and relatively normal-looking the next, she was careful to make allowances. He was, after all, adjusting to the loss of his mother.

"She'd formally ask if there was anything he wanted to talk about, and he'd thank her politely and say no. Discreetly, she'd change the subject. She stopped coming by unannounced. The two times she'd dropped by spontaneously had been distinctly unsuccessful. She now made sure that Fredrik was expecting her.

"Their familiar patterns, initially comforting, began to feel glaringly inessential. The fact was that they didn't need to eat at the dining room table anymore, or escape upstairs after dinner, or deal with Dee-Dee's daily dramas. They rattled around the house, revolving rather awkwardly around nothing in particular.

"Naturally, change was inevitable; they'd expected this. Ironically, adjusting to the freedom of fewer responsibilities found them seeing less of each other rather than more.

"With Dee-Dee gone, Fredrik began to see Pamela in a new light. He was bothered by things that hadn't bothered him before. Small things, like the way she chewed on her cheek when she was reading. Her long, rather melancholy face. His mother had called her horsy, but Fredrik had refused to see it at the time.

"There was a slackness to Pamela's body. Like Fredrik, she was tall and slim and looked good in loose clothes. But she lacked the kind of dynamism that his mother and ex-wife, for all their prickles, had had in spades. She had a tendency to slouch, which made her shoulders slightly round and her chest concave."

TELL ABOUT THE HORSES.

"It was in the area of the chest that things eventually got out of control. Pamela had the kind of long, free-ranging breasts that seemed forever to be loose in their harnesses. It puzzled Fredrik that she wore a brassiere at all, given that the ones she chose did nothing to shape or support her. Her breasts would dip in and out of their long white hammocks like the heads of horses dipping in and out of their feedbags.

"The sight made Fredrik nervous. There was too much slack in the works. It left him with the feeling of things unraveling. Dams breaking. Connections snapping. As if the breasts were not securely attached to their owner. As if at any moment they might snap their harnesses and gallop away.

"It was distracting to imagine a woman's breasts just taking to the road and galloping off. Like the furniture thing, it had started with an innocuous image in the back of his mind. But as background again became foreground, the image had grown more insistent.

"He now found himself suspended in Pamela's presence —waiting to see what the horses were up to. When he let himself glance directly at her chest, he would see two bobbing heads—sniffing the air, whinnying, chowing down.

"'*The horses are restless tonight*,' a voice would say. Or '*The horses are quiet; they must be feeding*.'

"He'd steal a glance at the bottom of the bags, checking for signs of nibbling.

"Sex was becoming increasingly difficult. The horses just got in the way.

"Life itself was becoming increasingly difficult. Along with the insults of the furniture, the mutterings of the pot ('*Make my day, Bucko!*'), the demands of the family and the complications of the horses, there seemed to be so much in the way of just living: the bills, the dishes, the shopping; the bathtub, the toothbrush, the laundry—the interminable logistics of it all. Everything was asking for something. It was *'read me, sit on me, pay me'*... *'fill me, eat me, clean me'*... *'use me, mess me, tidy me'*... On and on it went, washing one's body and cleaning one's cage, over and over and over. "

> Okay, stop. That paragraph sounded ridiculous even to me. There's no way Fredrik would say that.
> *Not without the hamster. You have to bring back the hamster.*
> Told you.
> *No, you said forget the hamster. But if you're going to start talking about cages, you're going to need the hamster. It doesn't mean the hamster was good. The hamster was bad. The issue here is coherence.*

DROP THE HAMSTER. THIS IS GOING ON TOO LONG. GET ON WITH IT.

> Right.

"Fredrik had to concede that while he did not miss his mother, the tyranny of the mundane had escalated dramatically since she died. He supposed she'd been something of a buffer. The tick-tock was now continual. He knew he'd done a laundry two weeks ago—how was it that he was already out of shirts and socks? Where did all the clean towels go? He found it perverse that he couldn't just brush his teeth once and for all and have done with it. He couldn't have the perfect bath, the ultimate laundry, the complete house-clean and call it a day. It went on and on and on. Even when one was tired to the bone by the ceaselessness of it all, still day followed night. Night followed day. Lunch followed breakfast. What was it all for? And what could a therapist possibly have to say?

"'*Ah, you are feeling trapped by the cycles of life, is that it? Like the dog who keeps circling, perhaps, and can't quite settle? Are you having trouble finding the right spot?*'

"'No. Well, yes—but *no.* That's not the point. The point is that I never get past the meaningless, on-the-way part to the real part: the good, the true, the beautiful part. Not some limping hybrid of this and that, everything bleeding into everything else... thoughts of cleaning the sink mixed with an old Beatles' song mixed with a mindlessly cheeping bird mixed with children scrapping somewhere mixed with the smell of oranges mixed with thoughts of Pamela...'

"'*So, you are feeling overwhelmed, perhaps? Your life has become unpleasantly crowded?*'

"'Yes. Brilliant. Thank you very much. That was not nearly obvious enough till you pointed it out. How could I have missed such a spectacular insight? You're fired.'"

SETTLE DOWN. TELL ABOUT TAKING ACTION. GET BACK TO THIRD PERSON.

Right.

"It was clear that something had to go, and given that Pamela was the most actual and detachable element, she went next. Fredrik prepared a brief, polite speech, suggesting some time apart—a month, or perhaps a few—and Pamela assented with a sigh."

> *(They always blame the horses.)*
> (That is a completely meaningless statement. And they do not.)
> *(Just saying.)*

"A step had been taken. Pamela time was now free time, and for a while the noise subsided. He could do whatever he chose, directed only by what he deemed worthwhile. The problem was that as time went by, it got harder to tell what was worthwhile. Nothing felt more important than anything else.

"Morning would find him in the vertiginous grip of option-overload, sifting through a million possibilities, incapable of settling on one.

"He'd sit down with a novel and immediately be distracted by the thought that fiction in the morning was frivolous, an escape.

"Nonfiction then: He'd surf the net for news, only to feel a wash of irritation. Wars, famine, viruses, global warming: they all had such an unfair advantage. As if life wasn't hard enough, you had to feel guilty for the luxuries of privilege. And privileged for the luxuries of guilt. Apparently a bad day couldn't be that bad if you were watered and fed. Besides, as long as the so-called leaders of the so-called free world remained intent on trading all hope of global accord for a game of Monopoly (or was it chicken?), there was really no point in following the news.

"And what *were* you supposed to do with the impossible but indisputable fact that you were on the last voyage of the *Titanic*? However Fredrik did the math, the ship was going down and the chances of turning it around were in the negative numbers. There were no lifeboats, nowhere to lower them even if there were, and the captain—*has anyone seen the captain?*—had evidently concluded, oxymoronically, that the solution to running out of fuel was to step on the gas.

"When he thought about it, wasn't mathematics just another way of finessing the finale? Was there anything substantial in his work beyond the distraction factor?

"Self-help then: He'd riffle through the pages of something that promised happiness, only to reject it as unscientific. Besides, they expected you to answer all those fluffy questionnaires.

"Creativity then: He tried writing, but the topics that sounded profound in his head became platitudes on paper. He tried drawing, but the lines were embarrassing—old familiar doodles of stars and moons, profiles of faces, breasts in feedbags.

"All right then, exercise. He couldn't bring himself to go to a gym, so he tried running. But moving fast made him feel like something was after him. Besides, he was too tall; he knew he looked ridiculous.

"Behind every activity was the gnawing suspicion that he was missing the mark. Or the mark itself was missing. How could he know? Nothing was properly hinged to anything else. Everything floated in its own little space, as if an order had been overthrown when his back was turned and no new order imposed.

"He settled for taking walks. Short, aimless walks that lengthened over time as he delayed his return to a house that felt cold and complicated. To avert the morning vertigo, he wrote lists, carefully numbered to synchronize his shopping with his walks. Lists created an illusion of order; crossing things off created an illusion of progress. And when the last item was crossed off, he was free to read novels—if he so chose—for the rest of the day."

TELL ABOUT THE NUMBERS.

"It was not long, however, before the general malaise began to infect the world of numbers. Lists, which had initially been stabilizing, now ceased to be reliably list-like. Since boyhood,

Fredrik had found refuge in numerical calculations. Numbers were his friends—reliable, predictable and until now, impervious to life's inevitable slings and arrows. But like everything else that had climbed on the bandwagon, numbers had begun to assume personalities. New personalities, as it happened; he had never really noticed the old ones.

"As he scanned the day's plan, it was impossible not to notice that sevens were wearing their caps backwards."

> *Sevens? Really? They were always so... what? Spiritual. And thin.*
> I'm not finished.

"Threes had sprouted ruby-red lips."

> *Well. We saw that coming.*
> No, we did not. Stop interrupting.

"Nines had taken to winking slyly and doing things behind your back, while eights, historically so aloof, had become excessively solicitous."

> *2008, my friend. Trauma will do that. 2009 was no picnic either.*
> We're talking numbers in general, idiot. And I'm not your friend.

"Ones—always the little guys—were suddenly full of themselves, and twos, in a hopeless attempt to look tweedy, had become unbearably dull."

The terrible twos—over-compensation at its worst, my brother.
Shut up. And I'm not your brother.

"Fours—historically plain and proud of it—had decided, to the horror of all things numerical, that they were funny..."

(Never, ever encourage a four.)
(I reluctantly concur.)

"... while fives, once so happy-go-lucky, had become insanely contentious. And sixes, traditionally so elegant and understated, had become transparently slick."

Like I always said, you can never trust a six.
You have never said that. Not once. Not ever.
Like I always... mmf.

"The novelty of new personalities was disturbing enough. But the prospect of what might happen when they began to interact did not bear thinking about."

Sixes and threes, man—I bet they have fun.
We're not going there.
No, seriously—maybe they'll multiply. Maybe we'll get a little eighteen.
I'm not listening. And it's never a question of maybe with mathematics.
We couldn't keep it though. We'd have to drown it. Or wring its little neck.
I'm not listening.
Yes you are.

ENOUGH. MOVE ALONG. TELL ABOUT MEDITATION.

"Easy to say that something doesn't bear thinking about. Harder, as Fredrik knew only too well, to not think about it.

"It was time to get a grip. He would learn to meditate.

"Meditation had always looked like a lot of work for very little reward. It had sat on his back burner for decades, one in the familiar series of last resorts that had never been exercised due to questions of sequence and merit.

"But the prospect of becoming a neutral observer—a constant among variables, as it were—held a definite appeal. And there were promising moments at first. Surprised by the novelty of being roped and harnessed after so many years of ranging free, his mind would lapse into a kind of lucid stupor—a simple awareness that wasn't cluttered by the usual mental commentary. This was apparently the object: awareness without the add-ons.

"Very quickly, however, the novelty wore off. The harness began to chafe as his mind remembered that the add-ons were what made life bearable. They offered hope, they promised that tomorrow would be better. They assured you that good things were coming right after you got past this messy in-the-moment part. The mental commentary explained how it all worked, what it all meant. Repetitive, yes. Predictable, certainly. But reassuring nonetheless.

"Being simply in the moment simply felt like settling for less. There you were on your zippy little mental speedway, looking ahead to the next big-city stop, and something was telling you to get off *now*, in the middle of nowhere. Right *here*, in this junky little backwater where nothing of interest could possibly be happening.

"Get off the train. Lose the tracks. Wander into nowhere-land. And do what?

"Occasionally he'd lose the tracks and feel erased—as if he'd either lost the ability to experience anything or the world had evaporated and there was nothing left to experience. It was like falling into the interval between tracks on an old LP. He could hear the faint, staticky hum of it.

"Episodes between tracks would alternate with caustic commentaries from the furniture.

"'*Well, you may think you're meditating, but you're not. Whatever you're doing, it's not what you'd call meditation. It's just a bunch of stale boring thoughts circling around nothing, going nowhere. Nope. Not meditation, no-siree...*'

"Ironically, it was the observer he had taken such pains to cultivate that ultimately did him in. He would begin to attend to his breathing, only to become irresistibly self-conscious. As he began watching himself, the observing part of him would split off to watch him watching himself, becoming in the process an observer once-removed. In stepping back to observe things afresh, a new observer would watch the observer once-removed observing the original watcher, becoming in the process an observer twice-removed. And on it would go—the subject splitting off to create a new object, over and over and over, till he found himself in an endless hall of mirrors.

"With the watcher watching the watcher indefinitely, Fredrik's mind was back on its zippy little speedway and happy once again.

"Fredrik, however, was not. As day followed night and night followed day with no apparent rhyme or reason, he fell into a boneless despair."

As opposed to a bony despair?
No. As opposed to nothing.
But the "less" implies...
Nothing. It implies nothing.

I blame the hamster.
I'm not listening.
Yes you are.

STOP IT. TELL ABOUT THE BEETLE.

"He'd be briefly motivated as he got out of bed in the morning, but the moment he finished breakfast, a dullness would set in. The same mind that could shift so dramatically into overdrive when he sat down to meditate would be flaccid the moment he tried to use it. Nothing held his attention. Even the furniture failed to get a rise out of him. He barely heard the couch; the table was a muted whine; the pot was just stupid. Nothing had the power to push him around anymore. He didn't care.

"Drifting into the kitchen one rainy morning, he noticed a large black beetle lying belly up on the counter. It was trapped in a crack between two tiles, and its attempts at escape had apparently got it wedged in permanently. Fredrik poked at it lightly with a chopstick to see if it was still alive. The little legs clawed frantically at the air, the body twisting from side to side in a vain attempt to right itself.

"Mildly fascinated, he poked at the beetle again. The sight was compelling, in part because the plight of anything trapped speaks to everyone and in part because it looked to Fredrik like the width of the beetle was actually a fraction smaller than the width of the crack. Which meant that if the beetle could levitate, it would be out in a jiffy. As it was, it could only heft itself from side to side and so was doomed to catching first the left and then the right side of its shell on the left and right edges of the crack. Something about this gave Fredrik a pang.

"'If you chose to embrace the chopstick instead of instinctively attacking it,' he announced, 'you might be a free beetle right now. Might, of course, being the operative word. You would have to be a very trusting beetle and I would have to be in a very benevolent mood.'

"The beetle's best choice was not clear cut.

"Fredrik put the coffee on and dropped some bread into the toaster. As he spread out his crossword, his eyes strayed again to the counter. Still struggling, though the movements were weaker. On impulse, he took a miniscule crumb of dried salami from the counter and pierced it lightly with a pin, which he dangled over the beetle's head. The beetle grabbed it with its front legs and shoved it greedily into its mouth. It chewed a couple of times and looked like it was waiting for more. Fredrik supplied it with a few more crumbs and a careful drop of water, most of which fell over its jaws and washed off into the crack. Then he went back to his crossword.

"Intermittently throughout the morning he'd apply the chopstick and watch the beetle flail. At lunchtime, he speared a morsel of potato from his soup, but it wasn't interested. He then tried a hard crumb of cheese that had fallen to the floor. It bit. Apparently it preferred its food hard and dry. Then Fredrik went out for his walk."

* * *

"Winter had apparently passed, though Fredrik had hardly noticed it, into spring. It was now early May, and as the days grew longer, his walks grew longer too. This was mainly for reasons of light. If he set out in the full light of early afternoon, it would be dusk by seven, and dusk was the worst time of day to be home. It was fine when the best of the light was yet to come and it was fine when the evening lamplight warmed things up, but it was difficult to be home when the last streaks of light were leaving the sky.

"He had resolved the dusk dilemma by stopping for dinner at the Crow's Gate Pub—a.k.a. Crawley's—on West Fourth Avenue. Here he was treated as a boring but harmless loner, known to return a nod, but not a great candidate for conversation.

"On his second visit, the pub had been full and he'd shared a table against the wall with an ancient retired professor named Weibel. After shaking hands and exchanging names, the professor had said, 'Very well then,' and looked purposefully off into space. Taking this to mean that a conversation was neither welcome nor required, Fredrik had gratefully left the professor to his rather active inner life.

"Equally grateful, the professor had taken to saving Fredrik a seat. He would hail him as he walked in the door and briskly pat the empty chair beside him. Fredrik would salute and sit down, leaving both of them free to think their own thoughts—and saving Fredrik the agony of casting about for a safe place to land.

"On the day of the beetle, he arrived at the pub a little earlier than usual and hesitated at the door. It felt strange to set foot in a bar before 4:00 in the afternoon. While he hesitated, a couple of young men came out. They recognized him as a regular and nodded. As they made their way to the street, he overheard one of them referring to him as 'the old guy who sits with the professor.'

"Fredrik understood perfectly that he was old to a thirty-year-old—he'd been thirty himself—but there was something in the young man's matter-of-fact tone that flattened him. Pretending he'd forgotten something, he turned around and headed home.

"It had been overcast for most of the day. Dark charcoal smudges were wending their way across a leaden sky as Fredrik trudged up Alma Street. Then suddenly, just as he reached 18th, the sun came out and warmed his back.

"His thoughts turned to the beetle. He had never been a pet person, but the thought of another life in the house, even a tiny trapped one, made him feel less alone. He hoped it was still alive.

"The pot stirred as he passed through the dining room, its mood more venomous than usual. '*Kill the beetle!*' it hissed. Fredrik ignored it. He dropped his coat on a chair and went directly to the kitchen counter.

"'*Of course I'm still alive. What did you think? I was going to just keel over and die because you happened to leave me alone all day? In case you hadn't noticed, I've already keeled over. Where's the salami?*'

"Fredrik speared a small chunk and lowered the pin.

"'*So, muchacho* (after a few vigorous chews), *where've you been all day? Water please.*'

"'Nowhere. Just out.'

"Fredrik lowered the dropper and squeezed twice.

"'*Nowhere I believe. Out I doubt. You haven't been out in years.*'

"'Excuse *me*—I was out all day.'

"'*Excuse* me—*you wouldn't know* out *if it fell on you.*'

"'Look, if you're going to just lie there making stupid comments, I'm going out again.'

"'*You don't know how to go out, Freddy-boy. You are stuck. Stuck stuck stuck. Oboy, are you stuck.*'

"'Am I deluded, or am I the only one who's mobile around here?'

"'*Mobile is a state of mind, amigo. Mobile you are not. Hey, I can move my legs too—See? Jiggledy-jiggledy-jig! Does that mean I'm not trapped?*'

"'Ah, so you admit it. You're trapped.'

"'*No, you're trapped. I was making a point. Trapped is a state of mind too. I could only be trapped if I was human. Like you.*

Which I'm not. Thank God.'

"Fredrik turned away in disgust.

"'You'll notice I can get away from you, you pathetic insect. I don't see you exercising any choice in the matter.'

"'*That's because choice is not my issue. Here I am is all I know. You on the other hand are doing everything you can to get away—and calling it choice. Like I said, my friend, you're trapped. I'm not.*'

"Fredrik sat down at the table with his back to the beetle.

"'The fact is, you're not even real. You're a figment of my imagination. All you are is a stupid beetle stuck in a crack on my kitchen counter. I can't believe I'm even having this conversation. I'm talking to an insect. This is too Kafka for words.'

"'*Au contraire, mon frère—not nearly Kafka enough. Not a hint of morphage in your little world. Day-old life is what you've got. Your cupcake is baked, my friend. Your jello is set. You couldn't morph if you tried. Your goose is cooked. Your muffins are...*'

"Fredrik picked up the chopstick and gave the beetle a poke.

"'*Ouch.*'

"Then he waggled it suggestively over the beetle's body.

"'*All right, all right. You made your point. By the way, the pot has to go.*'

"'It feels the same way about you.'

"'*No doubt; I'm a threat.*'

"'Right. Let me guess—you're making the pot feel trapped.'

"'*No, that's what it's doing to you. Lose the pot, Freddy-boy. Your mother will never know. Too bad in a way—it'd be better if she could watch you smash it to pieces. It'd be more of a statement. Oh well, too late for that. Your mother's dead. Dead dead dead dead dead. Dead dead dead. Dead...*'

"Fredrik turned on his heel and went back to the table. The beetle trailed off into a tuneless little hum."

Bio—FJS—May 7
Reality Check—Dynamic Elements:

1. Arguing with a beetle—patently insane
2. Irritated with a beetle—clearly ridiculous
3. Sun hitting tops of trees—definitely real
4. Sound of traffic in distance—perfectly real
5. Smell of wet wool from jacket—real
6. Knocking on kitchen window—sounds real; investigate

"He got up and walked to the window. The branch of a giant dogwood was tapping rhythmically against the glass."

7. cont'd... Encroaching dogwood, wingspan thirty feet—definitely real

"He fetched a small saw from under the sink, lifted the window and leaned out. As he reached for the branch, he noticed a large centipede perched on one of its twigs, directly in his sightline. It was pale green, about three centimetres long, and temporarily stalled by the shaking of its twig. Gently, Fredrik released the branch. With stable conditions restored, the centipede resumed its journey. Plump and plodding, its little segments rippling, it looked to be heading for the end of the twig.

"Curious to see what would happen when it got there, Fredrik pulled up a chair and sat down to watch. It took a good half-minute for the centipede to travel the five or six inches of twig, then there it was, confronted with space. Fredrik expected that it would now back itself into a loop and turn around, or perhaps continue walking upside down along the underside of the twig.

"Surprisingly, it continued to walk out into space. When its first three sets of feet had left the twig, they shifted from the rhythmic plodding of the rear to a gentle swaying motion. As more feet became airborne, the swaying became more exaggerated. By the time there were only three sets of feet left on the twig, it was two-thirds airborne and pawing the air in huge semi-circular swoops.

"Fredrik was mesmerized. The little worm looked so vulnerable, leaning out and groping away like that. Was it trolling for food? Was it looking for another twig? There was something disturbingly perilous about the whole game plan—something far too random in the way it was casting about for something to get a grip on. As if any old thing would do. How chancy. How arbitrary. What if it fell on a dog and got whisked away in a jungle of fur? It might be taken miles from home and end up in a perfectly strange backyard. What if one of the robins in the branches above decided to swoop? It wouldn't stand a chance.

"A flower box full of red geraniums hung from the windowsill, high above the garden. Fredrik reached for the centipede's twig and pulled it slowly toward the box, then gave it a vigorous shake. The centipede lifted off and landed in a half-twist on a frilly green leaf. Then it righted itself and began another slow, methodical trek.

"This time it headed for the edge of the leaf, which dangled several inches over the edge of the box.

"Fredrik could watch no longer. He leaned out, sawed off the intruding branch and closed the window. Then he broke the branch into kindling and carried it to the living room hearth.

"Returning to the kitchen, he glanced casually out at the flower box. The frilly green leaf was unoccupied, but jiggling slightly, as if a small weight had recently vacated the premises.

"Life.

"The beetle was still humming tunelessly from the counter. As Fredrik came into range, he made out the words of a twangy little song:

I'm at the end of my twig, oh yeah,
And I ain't gotta clue.
I'm at the end of my twig, oh yeah,
Got the centipede blues.
I kinda wanna jump,
But what if I bust my rump,
Get taken to the dump,
Turn into a soggy lump,
Ohhhhhh—I'm at the end of my twig, oh yeah,
Got the centipede blues ...

"'Shut the fuck up,' said Fredrik. 'I'm going out.'

"'*Sure you are*,' said the beetle. '*Oh yeah...*'

"'*Kill the beetle!*' hissed the pot, as he passed through the dining room.

"'Get a life, both of you,' said Fredrik."

***

"It was early evening on the first warm day in May. Fredrik took a windbreaker from the hall and strode out onto the deck. He was about to go down to the garden when something made him stop. A sudden heat rose from his chest. His throat swelled and his head felt too large. Also, his ears became uncomfortably hot.

"'*Enough*,' said a voice.

"'*Enough*,' said Fredrik.

"He turned and marched back to the house. From the shelf in the hallway, he took a hammer and a pair of pliers. He stopped by the bathroom and picked up a towel, then strode into the dining room, where he picked up the pot and wrapped it snugly in the towel. Moving on to the living room, he positioned the towel-clad pot on a stuffed leather hassock. Then he raised the hammer and pounded.

"When the contents of the towel were flat, he bent down to listen. Not a sound. He emptied the remains, towel and all, into a garbage bag, which he tied in a sturdy knot and placed by the back door.

"Pliers in hand, he now headed for the kitchen, where he picked up a clean coffee cup and wandered over to the counter. Not surprisingly, the beetle was playing dead. Lifting carefully from behind and below, he scooped it gently from the crack and flipped it into the coffee cup. Then he walked it outside and emptied it into a flowerbed at the far end of the garden.

"Finally, he went back for the garbage bag, which he carried three blocks to a can on the corner of 16th and Alma. Then he walked home.

"The house was quiet. Not a sound from the furniture. Not a peep from the appliances. Just the comforting creak of the old wooden floors and the faint swish of traffic in the distance.

"Fredrik left the back door open and walked slowly down the hall. When he reached the front deck, he opened the door wide and wedged in the doorstop. Then he wandered from room to room, opening doors and windows. By the time he got back to the living room, a soft breeze, fragrant with the scent of cottonwoods, was making its way through the house. Fredrik stood for a moment, inhaling deeply. Then he let out a long breath.

"There was a sensation he couldn't quite place. It was a little like having one's ears pop when one wasn't aware that they'd been blocked. He cocked his head to one side and walked slowly out to the garden.

"A grassy hill, good for rolling down when he was a boy, sloped gently away from the house. He picked a spot mid-way down it and stretched out on his back. A slight, nearly warm breeze billowed through his shirt, making his skin feel bare.

"As his body grew quiet, the faint background hum of the cosmos grew louder. Fredrik took a deep breath and looked up. In the next moment, despite the solid feel of the ground at his back, he found himself falling skyward. As he fell, he grew bigger and lighter, till in no time he had filled the vast dome of space all around him. Oddly, his chest, which felt a bit sore from all this, seemed to have grown larger than his body."

> *But not in a bad way, right? This is Fredrik, remember.*
> No, not in a bad way. I remember.
> *Good.*
> All right then, let me finish.
> *Righto.*

"Everything around him was moist and breathing, and the sky had turned an impossible shade of blue. For reasons he could not fathom, Fredrik's cheeks were wet and small puddles were forming in his ears. They made a squelchy sound when he wiggled his finger around."

> *Let's stop there, at the squelchy bit. Can we stop there?*
> All right. Want the last word?
> *No. I don't like endings. You?*
> No, I don't like endings either. Let's give them to someone else.
> *Okay.*

FOR GOD'S SAKE, *FINISH*.

> Don't push.

"From the grass far below, under a window box full of red geraniums, a small, pudgy voice was singing..."

I'm at the end of my twig, oh yeah,
But I still get about.
I'm at the end of my twig, oh yeah,
But I'm stepping out...

NEARLY BELOVED

NEARLY BELOVED

They have arranged to meet at a restaurant on Robson Street. Le Crocodile, 7:00 p.m. Having first met at the Crow's Gate Pub (a.k.a. Crawley's—a name she finds too creepy to pronounce), Barbara wishes to establish her preference for upscale venues and fine attire. She is wearing a short black dress, sleeveless, with bare legs. She will arrive a little late to give Kendall the full effect. The window table has been chosen in part for its sightline: he cannot fail to see her as she walks across the floor.

The evening is beautiful, balmy for May, and the slanting rays of the sun add gold to Barbara's light, if not entirely authentic, tan. She's a little early—it is only 7:00 now—so she slows to an amble and window shops.

The young man ahead of her stops abruptly, without looking back, to adjust his hair. Knees bent, pelvis forward, he crouches rather obscenely before his reflection, stabbing long thin fingers into carefully tousled locks. Barbara veers around him with a scowl.

She reaches the restaurant at 7:05 and is about to walk in when she hears her name. "Barbara—Barb! Over here!" Kendall is on the sidewalk talking to a young-looking blond woman. (Barbara is a brunette. She is also a few years older than Kendall and has been a bit coy about her age. She will disclose it when the time is right.)

Kendall has his hand on the woman's arm and they're both smiling widely in her direction. The woman is very tanned.

Barbara feels a wave of irritation. This was not the plan. Kendall should be inside the restaurant by now, waiting for her. Not out on the street with some blond woman. She would like to turn around and do this bit again, but the die, as they say, is cast.

She composes herself and returns their smiles.

The woman is clearly an old girlfriend—well, they both have pasts—and she takes Barbara's hand in both of her own, releasing her with a friendly, conspiratorial squeeze. Hers is clearly the role of advantage in the situation: the woman who has been intimate with the man, knows far more about him than she does, has remained his friend through God knows what thick-and-thins... and, Barbara surmises, can't resist being a little smug about it. It is the role she would have far preferred.

As things stand, she will have to suffer the charms of her predecessor with grace.

The woman's name is Corinne. She is sparkly and bubbly and blue-eyed—the kind of woman for whom the term "vivacious" was coined. A rapid scan tells Barbara that Corinne is shorter, lighter and considerably more animated than she. Bouncy, though not at all serene. Undoubtedly a cheerleader in high school.

Barbara was not a cheerleader in high school—a fact she now mentions with pride, though at the time she was privately crushed at being overlooked. Her own quiet prettiness had been slow to mature.

Corinne has just returned from six weeks in Mexico, where she has acquired the kind of seasoned tan that despite her fair hair and complete lack of makeup, gives her an exotic edge. It has been two months since Kendall has seen her and they've been making a date for lunch.

After the introductions, Kendall says, "Tuesday it is then," and turns toward Barbara. "Doesn't she look *wonderful*?" He is holding the woman at arm's length, openly adoring her, as if he expects the entire world to find her irresistible. Barbara smiles and shakes her head, speechless before all the wonderfulness.

Corinne bubbles and demurs and tells him to just cut that out or what was Barbara going to think. "Looks like you've been getting some sun yourself, Barbara," she says, sweetly redirecting the compliment. "Unless you're a tube-ster like old Orange Man south of the border. They're calling him 'Peach-Man' in Mexico now!"

She erupts in giggles and gives Barbara the cutest little wink.

Barbara mutters something about the beautiful weather they've been having and how her skin is naturally dark to begin with. *Damn*, she thinks. *Damn damn damn.* She'd intended to be honest about everything, but there were limits. *Well, I did sit out on the patio today,* she reminds herself. *That counts—even if I wasn't directly in the sun.*

The evening has suffered a puncture. To say nothing of the plans for later. A part of Barbara's attention will now be trickling off through dinner, wondering if Kendall's attention is trickling off to Corinne. The prospect of endless speculating is beyond tedious. She has only known Kendall a month. And of course she would never ask. She abhors people who pester one another about their previous relationships.

The nagging question, of course—the one that will really steal her attention—is whether or not the relationship is entirely previous.

She feels suddenly, overwhelmingly tired. If she could fabricate a convincing emergency she would leave them to it and go home. Something urgent and unforeseen. She would be warm and sincere and apologetic, but she simply had to run... She had actually just dashed down to tell Kendall... Hadn't had a chance to call... (*Damn, why not? They both had cell phones...*)... So, and, but, she really had to go... Wonderful to meet Corinne, lovely to see them both, couldn't stay a moment longer...

The requisite emergency does not present itself; her mind has grown dull. Besides, she hasn't displayed a shred of urgency since she arrived. On the contrary, she has been serene. It all feels ridiculous now—the planning, the looking forward, the dressing up.

The wave of promise, such as it was, has crashed. In its wake is a mixture of stale ennui and extreme impatience. Topped with a strong desire to scream.

She will have to make the best of it. She will at least have to endure through dinner. Perhaps a migraine after dessert...

It is only now that Barbara notices something wrong with Kendall's head. She hasn't looked directly at him till this moment, and realizes with a start that he has cut his hair.

She is suddenly, irrationally furious. Why is it that every time she meets an attractive man he goes and cuts his hair off? It makes her wild. His hair was perfect, all shaggy and long down the neck. Now he's gone and got one of those preppy close-cropped hairstyles with little side flips and nothing down the back. His neck is actually *shaved.*

He looks ridiculous. What was he *thinking*? His face looks so much rounder now, so much more common.

This changes everything. His shagginess made him look arty and masculine—how could he just go and change his entire look?

"You've cut your hair!" she blurts. He smiles at her uncertainly, surprised at her tone. There is a shy question in his eyes.

Oh right, so now I'm supposed to tell you how wonderful you look. I'm supposed to tell you the haircut looks great. Well it doesn't and I won't.

"It's very short!" she says.

"It's *fabulous*!" says Corinne, ruffling the little wings above his ears. "You should keep it short, Kenny, it really suits you."

Barbara cringes. She is personally sparing in her use of superlatives and would never call anything fabulous, let alone a failed haircut. Nor would she ever shorten a name like Kendall to Kenny. Kenny is a name for the supermarket boy, or the neighbour's budgie. It is not a name you could have a relationship with.

As it turns out, it is Corinne who must run. She's meeting her folks for dinner and she's late already. It was just *dynamite* running into Kenny like this—she has not once called him Kendall—and she'll give him a call about Tuesday. And it was *so* great to meet Barb. "You look out for old Kenny now; he's a doll, but he's deadly! Hey, wait a minute! Kenny and Barb! Barbie and Ken!"

She backs away, rippling with laughter, then wags a finger at each of them in turn.

"That's so *cute*! Barbie and Ken! I *love* it! Take care now, you dolls!" and she bounces down Robson to meet her fabulous cute family for a dynamite dinner.

Stiff with rage, Barbara allows herself to be led into the restaurant.

No one calls her Barbie. *Ever.*

"Barbie and Ken!" She has been careful to avoid even the thought. In fact, she has been careful to avoid Kens altogether for this very reason. It was just that Kendall had come along so suddenly, and she had found him so attractive (before the haircut), so boyishly open, so obviously smitten with her. She had pushed the image of the dolls aside and always called him Kendall, even in her mind.

But now the name respells itself: "KEN-DOLL" winks on and off in bright blue neon on her inner screen. The images rush forward—nauseous little caricatures of the bland wide-eyed pair doing a grotesque soft-shoe; stiff little arms and legs on stiff little hinges, vacuous little smiles on stunned little faces...

How can you entertain even the notion of romance—however flat it has now become—with cartoons of Ken and Barbie parading across your mind? It feels creepy just knowing they're in there. She evicts them with effort, knowing they'll be back.

They are led to their table by the window. Barbara settles vaguely into her seat, smiling distractedly over her menu at Kendall. She is not actually reading the menu, nor is she listening to Kendall, who is still rattling on about Corinne. It is a warm night and she is sitting in direct sunlight. She'd requested the window table for its sightline, and been surprised that it was available. She now realizes why. The accumulated heat of an entire day has poured itself into her chair, and there is no blind to pull. Within moments, her upper lip is beading, her scalp is prickling and her bare legs are sticking to her chair. She has to lift each thigh separately to avoid making flabby flesh sounds.

She curses her decision to wear bare legs. With stockings on, her legs would be sliding smoothly across her chair. She tugs at her skirt, knowing it's too short to do any good. A glance at her lap reveals deep creases. Already! She'd forgotten about crepe. The black jersey would have been a much better choice. There will be creases across her backside now as well.

She feels another wave of fatigue. And impatience. Kendall's cheerful chatter makes her want to smash something.

At the mention of babies, she snaps to attention. What babies? Corinne, he is saying. Of course, *Corinne*, but what's this about babies? She's looking wonderful, he is saying—yes *yes*—considering she has had two babies in under two years. Two babies? Then she's married? *Yes*, he has just been telling her. To *Brian*—his best friend. They've been married five years, Kendall was their best man, wonderful people, never sees enough of them...

A wave of well-being spreads like a shot of Chivas through Barbara's middle. Of course, *Brian*. The *husband*. She's sorry, she was distracted. *Brian*, of *course*, the *husband*. And their two babies, yes, *wonderful*. Corinne *is* looking marvellous, without a doubt.

She feels warmly toward Corinne. In fact, she feels warmly toward the whole family. Looks forward to meeting them all...

They order their food and a bottle of red, which Barbara lets Kendall select. She feels light-headed and freshly composed, as if she's been hurled unexpectedly through a violent kink in space, and landed even more unexpectedly on her feet.

She gives Kendall her full attention.

The sun glides past their table and dinner goes flawlessly. Kendall is enchanted with everything—the atmosphere, the food, the music—and Barbara. After an extra glass of wine, they are laughing and holding hands. Over brandy and coffee, they are looking deeply into one another's eyes.

As the light fades, the evening works a miracle on Kendall's hair. The little wings are magically erased and the naked neck is darkened by shadows. When she cocks her head to the side, she can still see the face that attracted her so.

***

After the ritual tussle over who should pay, they agree to split the bill and make their way out of the restaurant. They walk for a moment in silence, savouring the afterglow of a memorable dinner.

But all good things...

As she tries to fall into step, Barbara is filled with fresh alarm. It has to do with the way Kendall walks—*platch! platch! platch!*—so heavily. How had she missed it? My God, the man was positively flat-footed!

Was it even possible to fall in love with a flat-footed man?

A pair of stiff-legged dolls reappear on her inner screen. Their wide eyes have narrowed meanly, their vacuous smiles become smirks...

Platch! platch! platch!

She feels a hand on her shoulder. "Do you mind if we stop for a moment, Barbara?"

He bends over and undoes his shoelaces. Then he stomps around for a moment and ties them up again.

"New shoes," he says, standing up with a smile. "I've been trying to beat them into submission, but the laces were too tight."

The dolls recede. Barbara returns his smile and they move on. *Actually,* she muses, *he has a lovely walk. Quiet, confident. Athletic, even.*

And the great thing about hair...

BRIEFLY A SIDEWALK

(Napkinalia # 2)[2]

[2]*Napkinalia # 2 is a version of "Exquisite Cadavers"—words scrawled on a bar napkin by several people, all of whom must use a particular phrase in their contribution.*

BRIEFLY A SIDEWALK

ONE

Just once, she said, *just briefly—a sidewalk instead of an eight-lane freeway. One little stretch where you're off the road. A pull-out. A couple of planks across the mud. Is that so much to ask?*

Sweetheart, he said. *You sound tired.*

TWO

The boy looks about eight or nine. He's in the front yard and he's still crying when we come outside. He's been at it for a couple of hours; we could hear him upstairs. He's got a steady rhythm going and he's pacing himself: slows to a whimper for a while, then gathers up steam; bellows for a while, then slows to a whimper again. Soothing in a miserable kind of way.

An impossibly large snot-balloon bubbles from his nose as we walk by. Dutch stops. The boy looks over and hiccups. The balloon pops. He slowly drags his nose across the back of his hand, still looking at Dutch. Dutch says, *It doesn't get better, kid.* The boy stares blankly, waiting to hear what else. Dutch walks on. The rest of us are waiting by the gate.

The boy squints after Dutch, head slightly cocked, mechanically wiping the back of his hand in small circles on the front of his shirt. He waits till we close the gate, then turns and gets on with business. By the time we reach the corner, he's back in full-bellow.

We cut across Third and Collingwood, then briefly, a sidewalk. The car's about halfway down the block. Nobody says much as we drive off. Everyone's thinking *Crap. It doesn't?*

THREE

They're restoring the dunes at Asilomar State Park, so you can only walk in designated areas. Narrow paved roads connect the halls and residences of the conference grounds. Here and there a short stretch of sidewalk appears on the edge of the road, then abruptly ends. *Briefly a sidewalk*, you say as we step up. We walk in silence for about ten squares. *Sounds like a title for something*, I say as we step back down.

FOUR

Sam once crawled six blocks home from the house on Point Grey Road. Strobing on something. *Probably PCP*, he said. *I found it in the freezer in a piece of foil, stuck to the bottom of the ice tray. Thought it was just some old LSD.*

He says the whole crawl took him three hours. *The curbs were problematic, especially going down—steep as cliffs, deep as canyons. You had to curl up and roll over sideways. Then a stretch of road, then briefly a sidewalk. The intersection at MacDonald took an hour and a half. Not to cross, just to work up to. Cars still swishing by at 3:00 a.m.* (He goes down on all fours.) *I got stuck looking both ways.* (Swivels his head from left to right). *Had to wait for a car to go by so I could cross. Then a car went by but I wasn't ready so I had to wait for another one. Then I wasn't ready again. This went on for some time. Then there were no more cars. My whole system went out the window. I thought fuckit, no more cars. Then I thought hey, no more cars. So I crossed.* (Lopes across the floor like a lopsided crab.) *Made it to the far curb—easier on the ascent—took a few minutes to find my coordinates. Cheered up when I realized I was past halfway.*

He crawled through Tatlow Park and came out on Third Avenue, covered in leaves and dirt. (*Lucky it wasn't raining.*) Then he dusted himself off and did the last few blocks in under an hour. *Sometimes you just have to finish the night in your own bed,* he said.

FIVE

I dream of sidewalks, Marta says. We're stopped at the light on Fourth and Vine. *Neat rows of concrete squares, stretching ahead forever. In my dream, I'm half-flying, half-dancing, and I always step on the cracks. I try not to; I try to step in the middle of the squares, but I never do. You know how the plug on a Mac gets that little magnetic tug when it's close to the socket? That's how it is with my foot. It gets this little magnetic tug when it's close to a crack. Then whoom, down it goes. The really strange part is that just as I'm lifting off, the crack bends and makes a cracking noise. (A crack cracking—ha—only in dreams, Bella.) I can never look back, so I never know if it breaks in half or just fractures. Sometimes the noise sounds painful. Other times it sounds satisfying—like popping bubble wrap.*

We find a spot and park the car. Between the road and the restaurant, briefly, a sidewalk. Marta gives me a nudge and I turn. She grins, then lifts her knee and steps down hard on a crack. *Mothers,* she says. *Always a bit of a love-hate.*

BARRED

BARRED

We all do it, I guess. We go along thinking that the people we see every day must be living pretty humdrum lives. If they're showing up in my little day, what could be special? Take old Howard in the corner there, with his baggy pants and that moth-eaten cardigan he always wears. Just try to imagine he's something special. He comes in every day at the same time, has his two half-pints and leaves at 6:00 p.m. sharp. Barely says hello or goodbye and never looks right at you, he's that shy. But Professor Weibel told me the other day that Howard knows more about fly-fishing in BC than anyone else in Canada. Even wrote a book about it. And there he sits, kind of faded-looking and musty-smelling, hunched over his beer like any other regular at Crawley's. You serve him every day and you'd never know he was nearly famous.

So in a way, I don't feel too badly about what happened with Seth Stoker, but in another way, I feel a bit bad. It's not that I'm responsible, but I keep thinking if I hadn't been so glued to the notion that my job at Crawley's was just another detour in my day, maybe I'd have done something different. And maybe Seth would have done something different too.

It was early afternoon last Thursday when he came by. The lunch crowd was already gone, just a handful of regulars sprinkled against the walls. The thing is, Seth was barred from

Crawley's over a year ago and this was his first reappearance in all that time. Normally, people get barred for a month or two, six at the most, but with Seth it was terminal.

Seth is the worst kind of anti-social. He's a wiry little bundle of fury with a mean face and a permanent grudge against the world. If there's a woman sitting next to him, he'll start in on women. If there's an Aussie, he'll start in on Aussies. Or Germans, or Brits, or Asians, or Jews. If it's just some regular working stiff, he'll find out what they do and pick on that. How anyone can get all worked up about roofers is anyone's guess, but Seth will do it. Anyone he sets his sights on is going to become the scum of the earth. He's a one-trick pony that way.

So he'd finally jumped on one too many customers and got himself barred for life. Which is why it was such a surprise to see him walk in last Thursday.

He comes in, cocky as you please, and slaps his money on the bar like he's been doing it right along. The weird thing is, he's wearing a pair of dark glasses and a goofy woman's wig that doesn't even match his moustache. So it takes me a moment to remember he's barred. I mean you know it's him right away. His scowl is carved so deeply in his face there's nothing for a smile to hang onto, though he's giving it his best shot.

I'm a little dozy, but I do remember in time that I'm not supposed to serve him, so I tell him I'm sorry, as politely as possible, but I have to ask him to leave.

Well I'll be damned if he doesn't go all innocent and bewildered, like I must be mistaking him for someone else. I let him rave for a minute, then I give him the eyebrow.

"Come on, Seth," I say. "You know you're barred for life. You can't tell me you've forgotten. Now do us all a favour and scram, okay?"

Well. Now he gets righteous. He tells me I've got it wrong, he's not Seth, he's never heard of any Seth, and what kind of country is this if a man can't walk in off the street to a bar he's never been to before and order a beer like any other normal human being? As if he actually thinks he can shame me into falling for the disguise.

The thing is, it was so obviously Seth at first sight that I didn't even register "disguise." I just looked at the wig and thought, *Man, you'd think a person would at least try to match their moustache.* It had those bunchy little sausage curls, for God's sake, like an old lady's. And it didn't even go down to his neckline. Well, I can't help it, I start laughing. I say, "Seth, give us a break. You can't possibly believe we wouldn't know you under that goofy wig. Now get on out of here!"

A couple of the guys against the wall start yukking it up too, calling to Seth that he's going to have to do better than that for a beer at Crawley's. He finally gets that it's not happening.

Now if this were later in the day and Seth had put a few away already, we might have seen some action. The night he got dragged out for keeps, he wasted every beer glass and ashtray within flailing range from the bar to the door. Then he kicked all the outside planters over, just to reinforce his point.

But you can tell he's not warmed up yet. He hasn't had his first beer of the day by the looks of it, and though he'd clearly like to torch the place, you can tell he doesn't have the fuel. He gives the guys a half-hearted shrug—you can't blame a guy for trying—throws a couple of lame obscenities over his shoulder, and hits the street.

And that's that. A couple of times through the day I find myself shaking my head at that disguise. It's pretty strange, a guy going to all that trouble just for a beer at Crawley's. It makes me wonder if he's barred from Harvey's and Jiminy's too—the other bars on Fourth Avenue. But all in all, the incident is not much more than a moment's entertainment in a ho-hum day.

The TV goes on at 6:15 for the hockey game and we catch the tail end of the news. It turns out a woman has just been murdered by her husband in a Richmond trailer park. The man is an American who'd been deported from Canada six months earlier for illegal possession of firearms, assault with a deadly weapon—domestic squabble, no charges—and working without a permit. He'd re-entered Canada two days before and attempted to renew his liaison with the Richmond woman, who'd made it clear, according to neighbours, that she wanted nothing to do with him.

The neighbours reported hearing shots from the woman's trailer at around 5:00 in the afternoon. When two of them went to investigate, they were ordered at gunpoint to remove the unconscious woman and take her to hospital. The woman was placed on a picnic table till the ambulance arrived, and she died in Emergency an hour later. Police had been on the scene since 5:30, and the media had just got set up in time for the broadcast.

You have to picture this now: the camera is on the front of the trailer as the broadcast begins. The police have it surrounded and they're talking on the loudspeaker, trying to persuade the man to give himself up. Then suddenly, right in front of the camera, the man comes flying out, firing in all directions. And damned if it isn't Seth, in that same stupid wig and dark glasses. Then *blam!* He's down. The police nail him right through the head and he's dead on the spot.

According to neighbours, he was pretty tanked up and crazy. One man said he kept shouting that no one had the right to kick a man out—not out of his house, or the country he was living in, or anywhere else. He'd been kicked out of one too many places one too many times and he wasn't going to take it anymore.

It was a shock, to put it mildly, watching Seth get blown away like that, when he'd been right here in the bar just a few hours before. But the thing I can't stop thinking about is how we all just figured that disguise was meant for Crawley's. No one knew the guy was deported, or packing a gun, or mad enough to kill his ex-wife. Nothing that big ever happens in my little world, right?

And I thought about it. Not that it does any good, but I thought, who knows? Maybe if I'd bent the rules a little and given him one for the road—just to show there were no hard feelings—maybe he wouldn't have felt so kicked out of everything. Maybe he wouldn't have had to go out and shoot someone.

I mean I'm not exactly losing sleep, but it's crossed my mind.

BIG SPIDERS

(Napkinalia # 3)

BIG SPIDERS

I'm writing on a bar napkin. *Crap.* Can't believe I forgot my notepad. I'll go through this stack in no time. Gabe will be pissed.

Assuming I can write at all, that is. I only ever write on the yellow pad. But I refuse to go home. I'm too obsessed. Besides, I'll lose my thread if I don't write now.

(Kristina just smiled at me.) (Vaguely.) (Which is not why I'm obsessed.) (For a change.)

I'm obsessed because I'm acutely aware of an aspect of being human that's so constant and fundamental, it feels weird to me that it isn't a subject of conversation right here, right now, in Crawley's Bar. And everywhere else all the time, for that matter.

Put simply, I'm acutely aware of the boundless ocean of awareness itself. Big-A Awareness. It lurks in the background behind all my activities. Behind all the containers I pour myself into from moment to moment. It lurks behind everything that gives me a shape. Big Awareness, the Great Lurker.

I feel it as an amoeba-like latency, an unruly ocean of infinite possibility, biding its time in my back room. Ominous, formidable, darkly beckoning. It conjures up Jonathan Franzen's image of a Midwest thunderstorm: "big spiders in a little jar."[3] Only

[3]From *The Corrections,* page 358, by Jonathan Franzen, HarperCollins, 2001

the jar in this case is infinitely vast, the spiders correspondingly enormous. They crouch in the back room, waiting for the lid to come off. Waiting to leak or seep or sneak through some hidden trapdoor and flood the room I live in.

With it is a chronic background dread, a fear that if I don't pour myself into this or that—read a book, write some words, or at the very least, think a bunch of thoughts—I'll fall into this ocean of shapelessness and lose all sense of definition. I'll be ejected from the safe confines of my predictable foreground world, where all the familiar experiences live: the sensations and tastes and textures that confirm my sense of who I am: Boris (Beets) Niles—man, poet, lover.

I live in this foreground world. I depend on it for my orientation, my ability to navigate through a day. It supports my belief that I am a separate, cohesive individual.

But I'm haunted by the knowledge that foreground can't exist without background, any more than weather can exist without sky. The existence of the one necessarily implies the existence of the other.

(Or does it? Is this just dualism doing its thing? Creating the usual language traps? Are foreground and background anything more than convenient distinctions invented by the mind? Where does foreground end and background begin?)

(Oh shut up, Niles. It's a relativity thing, You could just as easily call it close-up and distant. Or near and far. Don't get distracted by the words. They're all traps.)

The point being, whether or not it exists in any objective reality *(ha—as if)*, I restrict my attention to the foreground. The close-up. And I keep my settings on "busy."

Still, I'm haunted by implications. Something whispers that I'm only living half a life. And the half I'm living is coming at me way too fast. I'm on the down escalator trying to run up, but no matter how fast I run, I stay in the same spot—always a little agitated, a little hungry, a little lost.

What to do? The logical solution would be to check out the background. Be adventurous, Niles—explore this vastness that breathes so continually down your neck.

Easily said. Unhappily, when I do stray, accidentally or intentionally, into this formless background, I recall all too quickly what the foreground commotion is doing for me:

It's protecting me from the intolerable experience of being a personality: a rabid consumer of ego-supplies with a curiously cruel capacity for self-awareness. A capacity that leads perversely to the realization that despite my hard-won knowledge that all my yearnings are ultimately doomed, still there will never be an end to yearning. (*Oh, Kristina...*)

It's protecting me from my meanness, my ugliness, my judgments about my looks and my smarts, my uncertainty about my lovability and my capability.

It's protecting me from tasting the certain knowledge that I'm not built to last, that no matter what intimations I may have of after-states, I still face irrevocable loss when I die. Everything as I know it, *gone*.

It's protecting me from the unbearable taste of my separateness, my chronic disconnection from life, within and without. It's creating that wall of white noise that distracts me from my deep sense of meaninglessness, from my feeling of being locked in and locked out at the same time—trapped on the surface of my life, nose against the glass, dimly aware that somewhere a feast is going on.

Somewhere I'm *not*.

Extreme irony, given that this foreground commotion is also the cause of my chronic disconnection.

What could be more insane? My mind incessantly constructing a wall of white noise to distract me from the dreariness of its incessant constructions. Stale solutions continually reproducing the same stale problems, locking me in to a life in the shallows. A life that had one school of existentialists believing that suicide was the only logical cure for the human condition.

I look in vain for a consolation prize. What do I get for taking these pains, subjecting myself to a glimpse of the background?

Most of the time, a convincing argument for staying in the foreground. The whispered suggestion that it's probably best to just keep up the clatter. The implicit judgment that I'm worse than pathetic if I can't take the heat. After all, everyone else (mostly) seems to be staying alive.

I circle my jar of spiders...

At some point it occurs to me that circling the jar is quite possibly the worst of it. It's so neither here nor there. I give up. Out of sheer exhaustion, I take off the lid and slide in. What else is there to do? I tell them to go ahead, eat me alive.

They're only too happy to oblige. The white noise gradually subsides as they set to work, sucking the sweet, juicy marrow of hope from all the bones of my constructions.

(Somewhere a feast is going on…)

One by one the structures collapse, until all hope is gone and I'm alone in the rubble.

I know this place. It's flat and empty and dead. There's nowhere left to run and nothing left to hide. I'm the little tin soldier who took off his suit and discovered there was nothing inside. Just emptiness, tinged with remorse: sadness for having invested so much in his suit.

* * *

After a long while, I notice the quiet. Bleak, but oddly relaxing. No straining, nothing to hold up. There seems to be something left of me as well, though I'd be hard pressed to give it a name.

It finally dawns on me that I've made it through the switcheroo. Background has become foreground. I'm now the thing I was running from—the formless ocean of awareness itself.

My sense of an impending thunderstorm has evaporated. Must have been a feature of life on the run. Now the spiders are all over there, where the foreground used to be. They look small and hectic from here, more like ants. Noisily milling about.

Me, I'm the emptiness inside the jar, though the jar itself seems to have vanished.

I'm just space now. Peaceful and quiet and vast.

I like this place. As always, I resolve to remember what a relief this is. I vow to bring myself to the feast more often.

As usual, I forget and get trapped outside again, circling the jar.

THE WEIBEL TREE

THE WEIBEL TREE

Bar Log, Crawley's, September 13

Professor Weibel died last night. Or early this morning; we don't know yet. Robert found him in the alley behind Crawley's at 6:00 a.m. Robert is the chef and daytime cleaner at Crawley's. He'd come in early to scrub out the kitchen and make his lasagne special.

"I figured he must have come in early too," Robert said. "By mistake, I mean." The professor can get quite muddled. "He was sitting in the orange deck chair, looking the way he usually looks when he's napping. You know—head back, mouth open..."

There are three old deck chairs in the back alley that we use on breaks when the weather's nice. Usually someone folds them up and tucks them behind the Smithrite when we close, but sometimes they forget. The professor always goes out the back way, so he knows they're there.

"My guess is that the orange one was left out," Robert said, "and he decided to have a little nap before walking home."

According to Robert, he was wearing the same brown suit he wore yesterday—well, pretty much every day—with the same blue shirt and brown tie. All his clothes are loose on him, so there must have been a time when he wasn't so thin. His white hair was sticking out in all the usual places and his legs were crossed high up in the usual way, with his brown fedora perched on the top knee.

"Not jiggling, though," said Robert. "But then he doesn't usually jiggle when he's napping, so I didn't think anything of it."

The professor's colour was about the same too, as far as Robert could tell, though you wouldn't ever say he had real colour. He's always pale as a sheet because he never goes outside, except to walk the two blocks to Crawley's.

So Robert just assumed he'd got the time wrong. "Though admittedly," he said, "four hours early is a little unusual." When he called out, "Good morning, Professor," and got no response, he wasn't concerned. It was balmy for mid-September and the professor looked comfortable.

He was about to head inside when one small detail caught his eye: The professor was clutching a can of Heineken. This in itself was not unusual; he always takes a Heineken home for his nightcap and brings back the empty the next day.

"But the odd thing was that the can was still sealed," Robert said. "If it hadn't been for that one detail, I might have left him to nap till we opened."

Feeling a bit spooked, Robert grabbed the top of the can and tried to wiggle it out of Weibel's hand.

"Couldn't budge it," he said, "Even when I tried a little force. More to the point, the professor did not wake up. That's when it hit me: he must have had a heart attack or something."

The thing is, no one ever takes a beer from Weibel's hand without waking him. Even when he stays till last call and we're clearing off tables, he never leaves Crawley's without draining his glass. And he doesn't take kindly to having it removed if there's so much as a drop left in the bottom.

So Robert called 911. The medics arrived in under five minutes and pronounced the professor dead on the spot. It was very sad news, and it has been a sombre day at Crawley's.

Bar Log, October 15

The problem now is that no one knows how to deal with Olivia. According to her, the professor's death is all our fault and she's threatening to sue Crawley's for not "serving it right."

Olivia is the professor's sister, and though nobody wants to say it out loud, we all think it's the other way round: It seems much more likely that the professor would still be with us if she hadn't meddled so relentlessly in his affairs. Anyone witnessing the fallout from her so-called interventions could see that they were counter-productive—if not downright cruel. They happened twice a year, and it took him a good six weeks to recover every time.

I was tending bar and happened to have my eye on the door when Olivia made her first entrance. You could tell by the set of her jaw that she'd expected to thrust the door open with one arm and sweep on in. And you could feel her irritation when the door did not comply.

It was obvious that this was her first visit to Crawley's because everyone knows the door is on a heavily loaded, slow-release spring, and therefore not amenable to thrusting. Unless you're a very big person leading with a very heavy shoulder, you need to push with both hands. Olivia is shorter and even thinner than the professor, and has no shoulder to speak of.

Not to be daunted, however, she stepped back, gathered her strength and gave it her best. The door opened slowly, as it always does, and as soon as it was wide enough, she squeezed in sideways. She looked manically around the bar for a moment or two, then bustled imperiously to the self-serve counter.

"*Where's Walter?!*" she shouted in my direction.

It was only mid-morning and the bar was quiet. At the sound of her voice, every face in the room turned away, anticipating pain. Then they all turned back, not wanting to miss any. The Bar Confrontation is as close as it gets to an indoor blood sport.

"Walter who?" I asked pleasantly.

"*Weibel!*" she yelled.

Interesting, I thought. We never imagined he had a first name. But of course he would.

"Ah, the *professor*." I smiled politely and glanced across the room to his table against the wall.

"Professor Weibel," I sang. "Someone to see you, sir."

Following my gaze, she turned on her heel and strode briskly to the table, where Weibel was visibly quaking. After very few words, he rose from his seat and the two of them marched out of the bar.

Gossip abounded for days as to whether she was a wife or a lover or someone he owed money to. No one thought for a moment she might be a sibling—though we later agreed the resemblance was striking.

He was gone for three weeks that first time, and I will never forget the day he came back. We open at 10:00 a.m. and he had been waiting out front on the ledge at the top of the stairwell since 9:00. The ledge is even with the flowerbed, which tends to spill over, so he usually takes a moment to brush himself off before coming in.

Not, however, on this day. On this day, he sprinted to the bar the moment the door opened, a ten-dollar bill in one outstretched hand and a clump of flowerbed dangling from his backside.

"Morning Gabe," he said. His tone was urgent. "A pint of your finest, please!"

"Coming right up, Professor!" I made a little brushing-off gesture and pointed to his bottom.

"Ah yes, thank you," he said, and brushed himself off.

Robert appeared with the broom and pan and discreetly swept up.

"Good to see you back, Professor," he said.

"Very good to *be* back, Robert," said Weibel.

It was immediately apparent that something was amiss. The professor never orders full pints. He sips steadily on half-pints and paces himself. The bar is his living room and he likes to last all day.

No one could understand why he put up with his sister's tyranny until we learned from Mike Styles that Olivia had control of his money. Mike had been a student of Weibel's in the "before-days." Like the rest of us, he thought well of him and made an effort to help him out when he could. He kept tabs on his legal affairs and managed the odd crisis—as when Weibel set fire to his kitchen curtains and needed help with the eviction notice. He had also inadvertently become the professor's Power of Attorney, and later, his Executor.

All pro bono, to Mike's credit. In fact, despite having an insanely busy practice, Mike has become the emergency go-to lawyer for almost everyone at Crawley's. He acts all snarly and snotty about it, but I think that's just a cover. Crawley's is his living room too.

It was well-known that Weibel's passion for the demon alcohol had long ago eclipsed his passion for teaching mathematics at UBC, and that this had led to his termination. Though he retained a tiny pension from the university, it was not enough, we now discovered, to cover his necessities and pay the rent on his basement apartment on Second and Dunbar.

Which brings me to our most stunning discovery: *The professor was only sixty-three at the time of his death.* We all assumed he was at least in his eighties. So in fact—and this is where age becomes critical—he was still two years away from collecting his Old Age Pension.

This, we later learned, explained his sister's hold on him. Olivia had control of their shared allowance from a very large inheritance and she would dole out just enough to make up for his shortfall. With nothing to spare.

The mystery remained as to how and why she had become her brother's keeper until Mike uncovered the details of their parents' will. Apparently their inheritance had been held in trust by the family's law firm for over twenty years. Their father, long since deceased, had instructed the firm to withhold all but a modest allowance—about $2000 apiece per month—and whatever funds were required for Walter's rehabilitation. Neither was to have access to their full share of the inheritance unless and until two conditions had been met:

One: Walter had been continuously sober for one full year and a day; and

Two: Olivia could legally prove that she had supported Walter's sobriety through a minimum of two formal interventions a year, until such time as Walter had met condition number one.

So in effect, though Olivia had control of their monthly allowance, Walter had become Olivia's keeper as well. Furthermore, rehab programs were extremely expensive, and though funding for these was apparently limitless, no rehab-equivalent fund had been set aside to support Olivia through her unhappy predicament.

Such an unholy bondage belongs only to a gothic novel, and they had been living with this stalemate since their mother's death two decades before. That is, from Walter's early forties till his early sixties. (Olivia was two years older.)

The mother Weibel had tried to remove the conditions before she died, but to no avail. Her husband had anticipated her "softness" and closed every loophole. He had never recovered from the alleged failure of his brilliant son, and never given up his naive determination to punish him back into shape.

Olivia, equally naive, though understandably resentful, had withheld all but Weibel's food and rent money in the hope that he would finally choose eating over drinking. Naturally, this meant that Weibel spent most of his allowance on beer. It was his only comfort.

Bar Log, October 30

Mike announced today that after much huffing and puffing, Olivia has decided not to pursue her lawsuit against Crawley's. This is partly because he convinced her she didn't have a hope and partly because she lost heart after pestering all the regulars. None of them would testify to seeing the professor drunk—*ever*—and they all made that crystal clear. Everyone knew the professor wobbled a bit, due to some kind of tremor, but he never lurched or took a tumble. And he was always a perfect gentleman.

("Weibels wobble but they don't fall down," Robert would say. Respectfully.)

Bar Log, November 15

Olivia came by Crawley's today, to everyone's astonishment. It's been two months since the professor died.

I didn't recognize her at first. Her jaw had lost that grim set and her white hair, which she always wore in a neat little bowl cut, was sticking out all over the place.

When I realized who it was, I half-expected her to yell, "*Where's Walter?!*" in the usual fashion. To be honest, I wondered if she'd gone a little mad and forgotten he was dead. But she didn't yell, or ask for Walter. She ordered half a pint, briskly but politely, then made her way to Walter's old table against the wall.

When she came back for a second, I told her how sorry I was for her loss, and how much we all missed the professor. She nodded a few times—rather dismissively, I thought—and tottered back to her table. (*Strange, cold woman*, I thought.) But then I noticed she was dabbing at her eyes with a napkin.

Bar Log, December 21

Olivia has been dropping by Crawley's quite regularly this month. Once a week at first, then twice, and this week, incredibly, every day. I find this bizarre. We all do. Is she dementedly thinking she can bring the professor back by frequenting his old haunts?

Mike says she's a wealthy woman now; apparently the inheritance was over a million apiece. With the professor gone, she gets it all... after waiting twenty years.

Another odd thing is that Robert keeps seeing her at the professor's old apartment. Robert lives on the same block. He assumed she was still clearing out Walter's belongings, but Mike says she's moving in. What makes this doubly weird is that she owns one of those fancy condos out at UBC. Clear title now, too, Mike says.

But I haven't even touched on the biggest surprise of the week: It turns out that Olivia is a professor too—or was until last year, when she turned sixty-five. Something to do with forestry management.

As Weibel's executor, Mike has spent a fair bit of time with her and he says she's not so bad. He actually sat down at her table yesterday and bought her a beer.

Bar Log, January 13

Everyone seems to have survived Christmas. We had a nice little New Year's party at Crawley's—nothing fancy—and I opted to work the bar. I generally prefer to serve than be served on New Year's Eve.

Olivia came in at around 9:30, wearing the professor's brown fedora. It felt a bit funny seeing it on her at first, but I have to admit it brought back nice memories.

"I thought Walter might like to be here tonight," she said.

Robert bought her one on the house and we had a little toast to the professor. Then someone said "Which one?" and everyone laughed. So we had a little toast to Olivia too. Who would have thought there could be two Professor Weibels?

Bar Log, January 31

I've just realized that Olivia has learned all our names. Professor Weibel (the first) did the same. There are people who have been regulars at Crawley's for years and never learned our names. Not that it matters, but it's nice when someone goes to the trouble.

Bar Log, February 12

We've been teasing Robert about having a new "girlfriend."

Ever since Olivia had a taste of his lasagne, she's been coming in early for lunch. I caught them having an animated discussion today about how not to wrap a sandwich. Robert is a stickler in this regard. He claims that "most people" (meaning *us*, if we're helping him out) don't have a clue. Apparently we "strangle the life" out of his sandwiches by wrapping them too tightly.

"They lose their freshness in half the time!" Robert says. "The secret is a light touch and a loose wrap—you *have* to let them breathe."

They went on to discuss the merits of waxed paper over Saran Wrap and how if you take a little time to layer the lettuce with paper towels after washing it, it will last three times as long. You could tell by their righteous tones that they were on the same page.

Bar Log, March 15

Someone has been messing with the flowerbed. We noticed a new plant today that looks more like a tree than a flower. It has a little wire fence around it, and the earth has been carefully tamped down to keep it upright.

The flowerbed is Robert's domain and he has been put out all day. To make things worse, he's convinced that three of his flowers have been stolen.

Bar Log, March 18

Robert just reported that his missing flowers were not stolen after all. They were resituated, but they're still there. Overall, he said cautiously, the garden is pretty much intact.

Bar Log, March 20

Robert caught Professor Weibel (the second) standing on the ledge by the flowerbed at 8:30 this morning. She had a water pack on her back—the kind climbers use, with a hose coming out one end—and she was watering the new tree. The garden faces south and gets the sun all day, so the soil dries up pretty quickly.

Robert said she was wearing sunglasses, a plaid headscarf and an oversized raincoat that looked like the professor's. He believed she was in disguise.

"Morning, Professor," he said.

"Why Robert," she said. "I was just..."

"... just passing by and thought you'd water our new tree? Brilliant. Thank you. Do you happen to know what kind it is?"

"Why yes, I believe it's an olive tree, Robert. Rather a foolish thing to plant in these parts, some might say, but they've been known to live through ten below."

"Ah. *Survivors*," said Robert.

"Well, one can hope," said Olivia, as she bent the hose and tucked it back in its pack.

"Harbingers of peace, too," said Robert. "And reconciliation, if I'm not mistaken."

"So I've heard," said Olivia. "When their branches are extended, they say."

As she made her way to the end of the ledge, Robert held out his hand.

"Walter would be pleased," he said, helping her down.

"Thank you, Robert," she said. "One can hope."

ACKNOWLEDGEMENTS

First, heartfelt thanks to the late and brilliant Tom Flemons for his inspiring friendship, exceptional hospitality, and generous bequest, which made this book possible.

Seasoned readers are like gold, and I have been blessed with several through the writing of this book.

Big thanks to the following for their keen eyes and kind support:

Chris Welsby
Heather O'Sullivan
Jeff Hesthammer
John Johnson
Judith Brand
Judith Plant
Kenya Gutteridge
Leah Hokanson
Lee-Ann Jaworski
Margot Sutcliffe
Nancy Boyd
Norah Wolfe
Sarah Deagle
Skai Fowler
Ursula Vaira

Finally, special thanks to the late Gordon Campbell and the late Grant Van Alstyne for their gifts of laughter, music and lifelong friendship.

ABOUT THE AUTHOR

Margit Hesthammar was born in North Vancouver and has lived on the B.C. coast all her life.

The Devil Spinners is her third book. An earlier version of the story *Big Spiders* was published by The New York Times in 2013 and the first edition of *Crows* was published by Negative Capability in 1984. Other publications include *The Stump Gump*, a children's book originally conceived by her mother (FriesenPress, 2021), and *Choosing Work Before Work Chooses You* (non-fiction, Write Room Press, 2013).

Twenty years in the hospitality industry provided Hesthammar with a ringside seat for people-watching. Serving the public was educational, entertaining and for her, the perfect complement to the writing life. It also led to many enduring friendships.

When work-related injuries interfered with serving, she dusted off her English degree and began a second career in adult education, most recently leading corporate workshops on clear, jargon-free business writing.

Margit and her husband divide their time between Vancouver and Gabriola Island.

Printed in Canada